LIFE IS FOR THE BIRDS

by
Richard B. Ruggiero

Illustrations by
Yvonne LaForge

PARADISE PUBLISHING

New Jersey

*This book is dedicated to my
friends and colleagues for
their helpful appraisals
and to the kids in room
203 for their constant
encouragement and
continuous
support.*

Library of Congress Catalog Card Number: 91-61672
International Standard Book Number: 9628933-0-7

–

Printed by
THE TOWN HOUSE PRESS, INC.
Pittsboro, North Carolina

CHAPTER 1

It was a beautiful, bright afternoon in the spring. The birds were chirping happily and flying from branch to branch getting reacquainted with each other after a long winter. The air outdoors was filled with the smell of blossoming trees as a light wind softly blew. Actually, from where I stood, the air was not as fresh, and the sun was not as bright, but there was a distinct aroma of cedar chips in the air. I'm sure you're familiar with the aroma of cedar chips; these fine nuggets of wood are responsible for giving a pet store its wonderful fragrance. Everyone knows how a pet store smells, but it doesn't seem to bother the people who work there, or the animals that live there either. Well, anyway, it all began for me in a little neighborhood pet store on the corner of Howard Boulevard and Main Street in the middle of a tiny town called Meadows. Lots of my friends celebrated their birthday in the spring, but a few of us celebrated our hatchday. You see, I wasn't born, I was hatched. My mother kept my egg warm for a very long time before I was ready to break out into the new world. I came out of a pretty blue egg. My sisters, cousins and other relatives also came from eggs, white ones, but not as pretty as mine - at least that's the way I felt about it.

If you haven't guessed by now, I'm a bird; not just an ordinary bird, mind you, but a parrot - a Macaw Parrot. Macaws are one of the prettiest birds in the world. My wings are colored with blue-green feathers and my breast is a mixture of red and yellow feathers. I am really a great looking young bird. My beak is curved downward and can crack hard seeds and nuts. My sturdy feet are designed to hang on to a perch during a strong wind. My parents came from the continent of South America and were brought to this little pet store about six months ago. Actually, they didn't know each other back in South America, but when <u>forced</u> to live together in the same pet store cage, they soon fell in love and decided to raise a family. So this is where it all began for me.

My family's roots are in South America, but like Bruce Springstein, I was "Born in the U.S.A." Now, this tiny little pet store in Meadows, California, was the only place I knew. It contained lots of my feathered friends and basic pet supplies. I was familiar with these surroundings and felt comfortable living there. The world outside was a strange new place I would get to know someday when I was older, but for now, the environment of the pet store was exciting enough for me.

In my cage there were five of us: my parents, two sisters and me. I was the only boy in the family, so naturally my parents spoiled me. And being first hatched (even though I was only a few minutes older than my sisters), I was the oldest and gave the orders and made the important decisions like who should ride on the swing and important things like that. My sisters were very agreeable, and never had a bad thing to say about me (at least not to my face). My sisters were cute little twins that looked exactly alike. It was difficult to tell them apart, so sometimes they would play tricks on me and pretend they were each other. This sometimes got quite confusing. We always got along well with each other, however, I always thought they may have been a little jealous of me because everyone knows that the male bird is much prettier than the female. Actually, experts say the Macaw is one of the few birds where the male and female look exactly the same, but I know differently.

Next to our cage was a strange looking bird. Mom called him Cousin Toucan. He also came from South America. He had a long colorful beak. He looked a lot like the cereal box "Froot Loops" bird. His long beak had several different colors on it. What a pretty bird he was. However, he had a slight problem when he turned his head to look somewhere. He usually banged his beak on something in the cage. His cage was a bit small for that long thing. Both my sisters used to laugh at him when this happened. Sometimes they would scream out loud and make him turn his head quickly, and poor Toucan would bang his beak again and again. I wondered if the colors of black and blue on his beak were natural or caused by my sisters?

Now, across the aisle from my cage were the strangest bunch of animals. They were born, not hatched like me. They had fuzzy coverings of fur, not feathers like me. They even had long furry tails. These strange creatures always stared at us. Did they like to look at pretty birds (they must have looked at me the longest because I was the prettiest), or were they especially interested in us for other reasons? I asked my father, and he told me that these furry animals were called cats. He told me to be careful; cats are mean and nasty, and they love birds. He also told me that one of his brothers back in South America was a dinner guest of a cat. Being young, and sort of dumb, I asked my father what they had for dinner. My father said that his brother was the dinner. I didn't ask any more questions after that, but always in the back of my mind, I was very careful when cats were around.

Life was sweet and full of excitement and activity at the pet store. I learned all about the other different animals. There were dogs, mice, hamsters, fish, gerbils, lizards, snakes, turtles, and even some spiders. The store also had a spider monkey. This cute little fellow had long arms and would hang from the highest part of his cage and swing back and forth all day long. His name was Bobo. He seemed to enjoy his life in the pet store the best of all and I was a little jealous of him. Sometimes the pet store owner would take Bobo out of his cage when it needed cleaning. He would let Bobo hang onto his shoulders like a little baby. It was such a cute thing to watch. But one time while his cage was being cleaned, Bobo ran and jumped around the pet store. He started to knock things over and make a real mess. I couldn't believe it when he started to open some of the other animals' cages. Puppies were running throughout the store, and those nasty cats were trying to climb into our cages. It was so funny when the store owner slipped and fell onto the floor when Bobo threw a broken package of bird seed on him. Before you knew it, Bobo jumped up and then started to swing from the lights which hung high in the ceiling of the store. It was very funny watching the store owner, who was still covered with bird seed, try to catch Bobo with a net. Once he caught him, however, poor Bobo was grounded. His days of hanging around the pet store were over. He wasn't allowed to come out of his cage anymore. Too bad he didn't get to open my cage. I would have liked to have tried out my wings to see if they worked.

CHAPTER 2

It was just great living in the pet store; I had everything I could ever want. I would have been content to live there forever with my parents and family. But the day came when humans started buying my friends. I couldn't understand why all of a sudden this was happening. I overheard someone talking about a holiday where humans gave presents to each other to show their love and affection, and it dawned on me that my friends were going to be these presents. Each day more and more of them were taken from their cages and put into small boxes. I watched in horror as the offspring were taken from their parents' cages. What was going to happen to my family and me? I started to worry, but my father told me that it was the law of nature. He said that once a young bird was ready and old enough, he would leave the nest forever and start a new life and a family of his own. I asked my father when this would happen to me, and he said, uneasily, that my time had already come, and I should be prepared to go. I was a little nervous about the idea of leaving, but I realized I was no longer a baby bird, and I was a bird ready to go out into the world and start a new life.

It was a sad thought leaving my family, but it seemed exciting to be leaving the nest to explore the strange, new, outside world. Having a chip on my shoulder, I figured that I should be picked first, because I was the prettiest bird in the store. However, the days passed quickly and I was still there. In fact, my two sisters were gone first. They were bought the same day by two little girl humans. These girls were twins like my sisters. How cute they looked carrying their little boxes that contained my sisters out of the store. I hoped my sisters would be happy in their new life in the outside world. I chirped a farewell to them as they left the store. But what about me? Why wasn't anyone going to buy me? Maybe I should act the part of a cool, sophisticated bird and that might attract someone's attention. So I put on the charm. Everytime someone came by, I jumped on my swing and rocked and rocked. I even started to chatter to get their attention. With all this effort, there were still no takers. I even tried to hang upside-down on the swing to make someone notice me. This did attract them, and they loved the show. I would rock and rock upside-down, and climb up and down the bars of my cage. Once I even fell off my swing to the bottom of the bird cage. It was disgusting. Everyone knows what's on the bottom of a bird's cage. The people thought I was great, even the pet store owner admired my work. It felt good to be appreciated, but I would have felt much better if I was bought by some sweet, kind human.

CHAPTER 3

The next day was the most horrible day of my life. Three humans came into the store: two adults and one mean, nasty teenager. This young boy had an evil smile covering his face from ear to ear. He looked about fourteen years old and was very annoying to his parents. I watched him as he walked around the pet store tapping the cages and the fish tanks. Signs said, "DO NOT TAP", but that didn't seem to concern him; he went right on doing what he wanted. He started to tease the little puppies by sticking his fingers into their cages and pinching their noses when they came by to sniff him. He started pulling on the cats' tails, but that didn't bother me. He even squirted the water bottle in the hamsters' cages and soaked the poor things. I personally would have liked that beast to try and stick his fingers into the piranha's tank; that would teach him not to mess around. Why couldn't these parents control their kid? All of a sudden I looked in front of me and noticed this kid's parents with the store owner. They were looking directly at me. They asked the owner how good a pet I could be. The owner said many nice things about how talented I was and recommended that they buy me. Oh, no! I didn't want to be bought by these people and live with that beastly monster. Not me, I'm too young to die! But it was too late!

The people decided to buy me, and that was it. I said goodbye to my parents, and got ready to start a new life in the outside world.

The little box they put me in had a few holes punched in the top. I was barely able to see any daylight. Luckily, the mother of this group chose to hold me. What a relief that was! I could just imagine Beastly tossing me around in the air. I hadn't been able to fly in the pet store because of the size of my cage, but I bet he would have no trouble teaching me the hard way.

It was a short ride home. I felt the car stop and my box being carried into a house. Once inside, the lady put me on a table. Then she left the room. There didn't seem to be anyone around - so I thought. All of a sudden, I felt this bang on the side of my box. Then another bang on the other side. This banging continued for some time. It felt as though someone was having his own personal ping pong match, with me as the ball. Back and forth, back and forth-I felt my feathers starting to ruffle. There was nothing left for me to do except to die. I figured this was the end. My life started passing in front of my eyes. Suddenly, from out of nowhere, the movement stopped and I heard this loud crack, and a louder, "OW!" I realized that whatever had happened to me just ended and the guilty human was caught

9

in the act. I had a feeling who it was, and from that point on, I wanted revenge. This was going to be an interesting relationship: Beastly and I were destined to be enemies.

Even though the box had stopped moving back and forth, my body couldn't get quite used to calming down. I still had the urge to bounce back and forth in the box. But that soon passed, and I wondered when these people were going to let me out. It was dark inside. I was hungry. I needed to stretch my legs. I wanted my mommy!

CHAPTER 4

The people kept me in the box for a few more minutes. I was very eager to get out, but I decided to play it cool. There was no sense in rushing out of the box and flying around if I didn't know where to go, so I decided to lie back and wait. Who knows what might be in store for me on the outside of this box. Things could be worse out there than inside. I figured I had the time. I had no place to go.

It took a few more minutes to compose myself when I heard the mother of the family call someone down into the room where I was. Then I heard a gathering of humans all around me. The string on the box opened and they removed the lid. There, in front of me, was another boy human, but this one was younger. "Not another one!", I said to myself. "How can I deal with two of these little monsters?" Now I really started to panic. The feathers on my back shot up like a porcupine's quills. I started to become very nervous and uneasy. This new child started to reach for me. I felt him put his hand around me. I had the thoughts of a tomato being squeezed for ketchup, and I was the tomato. But he surprised me. The boy was very gentle, and raised me to his lips and gave me a kiss on the beak. I couldn't believe this was happening to me. I noticed Beastly was sitting down on a chair by the table. He was making a disgusting comment of how gross it was to kiss a dumb old bird. I felt rather insulted. I wasn't old and not that dumb, but the boy who was holding me shouted back at good, old Beastly and told him to mind his own business. From that point on, I realized that I belonged to the nice little kid, not the monstrous Beastly. What a relief!

There was a fairly large bird cage on the other side of the room. The young boy walked carefully toward it and spoke to me gently as he opened its door. He said that this was my new home, and his name was Jimmy. He was happy I came to live with him, and we would have lots of fun together. But something bothered me as I entered my new cage: it seemed as though someone had lived there a while ago. Little Jimmy looked so happy. He said, "I hope you like this cage as much as Ralph did." Now, what did he mean by that?

After closing the door of the cage Jimmy looked across the room and noticed the large family cat. It was sunning itself lazily by the window. He stuck his finger sternly at the cat and warned it not to go near the cage. The cat seemed to smile at the boy in a sneaky sort of way. "This could be trouble," I said to myself, "and who was this guy Ralph?"

CHAPTER 5

The cage around me was an amazing sight. It was three stories high and had a large swing on every level. A condominium wasn't as elaborate. I felt rather proud to be the occupant of this beautiful living facility. Then again, I did deserve something that was equally as beautiful as me.

As I looked around, I saw a large feeder full of seed, a blue water dish on the lower level, and a tiny bell in the attic. As I moved around from floor to floor, I noticed this shiny object hanging from the main floor. I quickly jumped up onto one of the swings to get a closer look, and there standing right in front of me, was the prettiest bird I had ever seen. He was beautiful, with blue-green feathers and a long colorful tail. Could this be my roommate? I looked deep into the eyes of this fellow bird and asked him who he was. The bird only stared back at me with a dumb sort of look. I repeated my question, but still got no response. Was this bird deaf, or was he just stuck-up? I knew of some birds back at the pet store who thought they were too good to be bothered with anyone else, because they thought they were better and prettier than all the others. I knew I was prettier, but at least I was a friendly bird and tried to make friends. I was really starting to get annoyed with this fellow, and explained to him that if we were going to be roommates, we should at least try and be friends. There was no response from this stiff-beaked character. I was really beginning to become angry now. I put my nose up to his, and he did the same thing. As a matter of fact, that bent-beaked buzzard bunked noses with me. This made me furious! I spread my wings and started to ruffle my feathers. My opponent did the same. I raised a foot, and so did he. I opened my mouth, and he did the same. When I put my foot down, guess what he did? We weren't getting anywhere, so I offered a solution to the problem. I decided to go get a bite to eat, and maybe, after he thought it over, we could talk about our situation.

I was certainly hungry after all the excitement, so I went to the bottom of the cage to get a snack. Jimmy, my new owner, had already filled my dish with seed, so everything was all ready for me. Even Beastly was starting to become nice to me. I saw him grab a bottle out of a cabinet when everyone left the room. He was so nice to fill my water dish to the top. The bottle had a clear liquid in it. It must have been some sort of bird water, or at least that was what I thought it was. I noticed the spelling on the bottle. The letters were, "V-O-D-K-A". Vodka is an interesting name for special bird water. That Beastly was alright. Maybe I judged him wrongly. Maybe he was a nice guy after all.

As I started to eat the seed in my dish, I felt thankful for the humans that bought me. They seemed nice. Even Beastly was warming up to me. Now my only problem was that character on the other side of the cage. I would take care of him later, after I got a snack and something to drink.

The seed didn't seem to be too bad, but that water had a strange taste, like nothing I had ever tasted before. They never gave us water like this in the pet store. It must have been special parrot vitamins or something. I started to feel weird. My body didn't seem to be connected to my brain. I was becoming sick to my stomach. I decided to take a swing on the top floor swing to take my mind off of feeling sick. It was a great distance from the bottom of the cage, but I made my way up to the top by climbing and hopping from one side of the cage to the other. Once I made it to the top, I started to swing and swing. I felt so happy, I even chattered away as content as any bird could be. This was the life for me. But the more I became happy, the worse I felt. Here I was, a happy bird in a cage with a roommate who hated me. Now was the time to deal with that feather-head. I was ready for a fight if I had to, but once again, I felt as though I was going to become sick to my stomach.

I needed to get to the bottom of the cage in a hurry!

I didn't care about climbing to the bottom of the cage this time; instead, I pretended to be Superman and jumped to the bottom. I'm sorry to say that on my way down, I lost my balance and fell straight onto another swing. I tried to grab on to it, but missed, and fell to the bottom of the cage with a loud crash. My feathers were ruffled again, but at least I was at the bottom. After all, I needed to get to the bottom of the cage, and that was the fastest way to go. Anyway, it didn't seem to hurt me. As a matter of fact, nothing on my body felt anything. I mean, I was numb from my beak to my toes. I tried to get up, but my feet wouldn't listen to my brain. They just kept tripping over one another. I looked high up into the cage and saw that bird staring right down at me. I bet he was laughing at me. "Nobody laughs at me and gets away with it, I'll fix him!" I screamed. So I staggered to my feet and made my way up to the perch where my enemy was. I looked into his eyes, and he glared back at me. His eyes looked sort of glassy. He didn't look well at all. As a matter of fact, he looked a mess. His feathers were ruffled and he was swaying from side to side. Watching him sway made me feel worse, and all of a sudden the cage started to spin and spin. I felt dizzy. "It's all your fault!" I screamed at him. I started to peck at him, and he pecked back. I actually hurt my beak because we kept banging them together. What a hard beak he had. I pulled back and just then I realized that this must be that "Ralph" guy little Jimmy was talking about. "OK, Ralph," I said, "this is it - this cage isn't big enough for the two of us. One of us has to leave!" I started to squawk and scream at this bird. Louder and louder came the screams from my cage. They were so loud that Jimmy came out to see what was wrong. He saw me pecking and clawing. I was fit to be tied. "Calm down, Pretty Bird," he said, "What are you doing?" He noticed I was staring at the bird in front of me. "You silly bird," he said, "you only see yourself in the mirror. You have got to learn to get along with yourself". After saying that, he giggled and walked out of the room. Boy, did I feel like a dope. The whole time it was me in the mirror, not another bird. I began to wonder if I was related to the Dodo Bird or not.

CHAPTER 6

After making a complete fool of myself, I decided to take a nap. I was still sort of dizzy, so I sat on the nearest perch to me and shut my eyes, hoping things would be better when I opened them again. But, no such luck. My head started to spin and spin even worse than before. I started to rock and rock on my perch. What was wrong with me? I was healthy when I left the pet shop, why was I taking leave of my senses? Suddenly, it dawned on me - Beastly. That couldn't have been water he put into my dish. No wonder I wasn't myself. There was no time to think about that now, my first thought was to try to scrape what little dignity I had left and try to make the best of it. My head continued to spin and spin. I was hoping the cage would spin the other way to balance things out, but it didn't. I felt like I was on a merry-go-round with no way of getting off.

Feeling unable to do anything significant for the remainder of the day, I decided to sit as still as possible and to try to weather the storm. Beastly came into the room a few times to check up on me, and laughed each time he saw the dopey look on my face. He knew what he had done to me, and he loved every minute of it. My friend Jimmy also came in to check on me. He was quite disturbed about my solemn behavior.

"What's the matter, Fella", he said. "Aren't you feeling well?" He called his mom over to check me out. I tried to perk my head up, but the inside of it was beating like a drum. Boy, did I have a headache.

When Jimmy's mom came into the room, she looked real close at me. She noted that I looked real sick and thought I should be brought back to the pet store. I was shocked to hear this news. I didn't want to go back. I finally found a place to live with a nice boy, even if his brother was a "Beast." I mustered up enough strength to try to show them that I was alright. But as I stood, I lost my balance and fell far below to the floor of the birdcage. I was quite embarrassed, so I tried to get up. I began to stagger and fell face first into my water dish. Naturally, I splashed water or whatever that stuff in my dish was, all over everyone. Boy, did I really feel stupid then. These humans would now want to get rid of me for sure. Just then, Jimmy's mom licked her lips. Some of the water splashed her there. She tasted it again and again. "VODKA!" she shouted. "Who put Vodka into the bird's water dish? This bird is drunk!" Drunk? How could I be drunk? Birds don't get drunk!

The next thing I knew, she ran out of the room looking for "you know who"! The sounds of "smack" and "ouch" were like music to my ears. I heard Beastly say that

19

it was only a joke. His mother responded with another smack. She then grabbed the culprit by the ear and dragged him into the room next to my cage. She then instructed Beastly to look into the cage to see the trouble he had just caused. I was feeling a little better by now. The room stopped spinning and I was able to walk. But do you think I got up and walked around the cage like a healthy bird? Not me. I put this sad, beat-up look on my face, ruffled my feathers for effect, and started to stagger around the cage. I really out-did myself. I was the perfect little actor. This made his mom much angrier. She twisted the ear she had in her hand almost all the way around. I thought she might rip it off. He deserved it for playing such a nasty trick on me. I loved every minute of it. Revenge is sweet.

After my little performance, I felt much better. There's nothing like a good execution to fluff up a bird's feathers. But poor Jimmy was very upset by the whole incident. He reached into the cage and stuck out his finger. I immediately stepped on it, but I pretended to still be weak. He pulled me close to his chest and apologized for his brother's behavior. He then cleaned out the water dish and gave me a fresh refill. Then he patted down my feathers and kissed my beak. From this point on, I knew he would always be there to protect and take care of me.

CHAPTER 7

Things had quieted down for the time being. The family had gone into the kitchen for their dinner. I wasn't feeling up to par, because of my recent experience with Beastly and his mystery water. But that woozy feeling started to wear off. I figured I was do for a nap. So without another thought, I jumped up on my perch, stuck my head under my wing, and proceeded to take a short nap.

When I awoke a few hours later, I noticed I was completely surrounded by the entire family. They were all smiling at me and making comments about how cute I was. The mother also mentioned that I had been through a lot my first day. She looked directly at Beastly when she said it. I could see that she was still pretty upset about the "WATER" incident. Beastly cast his eyes down towards the floor and said that he was very sorry he had played such a nasty trick on me, and he promised he would never do it again. He really did look upset. I even started to feel sorry for him. Had I misjudged him? After all, boys will be boys. I was quite a prankster myself back at the pet store. I used to play tricks on my sisters all the time; not nearly as nasty as Beastly's pranks, but I was pretty bad. I remember the time I pretended to be a dive bomber plane and kept dropping bird seed on the girls' heads. It was all in good fun, and nobody really got hurt. Maybe I would give Beastly another chance. After all, we did have to live together under the same roof.

Jimmy mentioned to his mom that I needed a name. He said that he had been thinking about it for awhile, but hadn't made any definite decision yet. His mom suggested that the entire family write down some names on a piece of paper, and they could all decide together what I was to be named. That sounded like a great idea to me.

After the family left the room, I started to think of all the names I thought would be suitable for me. I already had been called Pretty Bird. That seemed to flow well with me. After all, I was a very pretty bird. Maybe they would choose a name like Gorgeous George, or Handsome, or Mr. Beautiful. All of these names sounded just fine to me, because after all, they all made sense.

When the family came back out to the room, they all sat around the dining room table. The mother took all the pieces of paper from each of the members and she proceeded to read them off. The first name she read was Macho Bird. I loved that one. It suited me perfectly. Then she read Smelly Bird. I had an idea who had suggested that name. The next one was Cutie Pie. Cutie Pie? What kind of name is that for a boy parrot? That name was definitely out. Another choice was Ralph 2. There was that Ralph name again. Who was this Ralph guy? His name always seemed to come up. A few more names on the list were read, but they still didn't seem appropriate to me or the family. One name that was read was Cat Food. Cat Food? Why would anyone want their bird to be called Cat Food? Upon reading this, the mother once again glared at Beastly. He gave a sort of stupid smile and said that he was sorry. This was the sorriest kid I had ever seen. His mother proceeded to tell him he had better knock it off. She also reminded him that Jimmy was still very upset over the loss of Ralph. Now things started to become a little clearer. Ralph must have been lost somewhere - but where?

Since the family couldn't agree on a name, they decided to try again a little later. So, with that, they left the room. I was alone once again, to do all the stuff a bird does in his cage. I thought to myself, "Now, what could I do?" I could swing on my swings, or I could jump around the bars of the cage. I could do some acrobatics, like hanging upside down. None of this seemed to be of any interest to me, actually, the thought of it seemed rather boring. Let's face it, life for a bird is boring. I was a social bird. I liked humans around me - except for, maybe, that Beastly.

Speaking of the devil, you will never guess who just happened to walk into the room at that very moment. Guess who? He was carrying a piece of food in his hand. He walked up to me with a very sweet look on his face. I was wondering what he was going to do to me. But to my amazement, he placed an object in between the bars of the cage and told me that this was a peace offering from him. He was really sorry for the joke he pulled before and he was offering this "pepper" to show his friendship. "What a sweet boy," I thought to myself. Isn't that nice of him to try to make friends with me. He did look very sincere, and the "pepper" didn't look like it would do any harm. So, being polite, I strutted up to the "pepper" and sniffed it. It didn't smell bad. As a matter of fact, it smelled very good. I opened my mouth and took a bite. "Not bad," I said to myself. This Beastly is alright. As I bit deeper and deeper into the "pepper", I noticed that it contained several, small seeds. Seeds! Wow! I just love seeds! Maybe these were "special seeds" for parrots. I bit into the seeds and started to chew them up. Then, in the back of my mind, I remembered that good, old Beastly once before gave me "special water" for parrots. Oh no! What had I gotten myself into?

CHAPTER 8

Here I was, with a mouth full of pepper seeds, wondering what I had gotten myself into. The seeds did taste rather good - like nothing I had ever tasted before. Should I swallow them and trust Beastly, or should I spit them out? But before I could answer my own questions, my mouth started to tingle, then it started to burn; then it felt as though it was on fire! My mouth became as fiery as a furnace. It felt like flames were jumping from my beak!

I finally had enough sense to spit the seeds onto the floor of the cage. They might have burned a hole through its bottom, but I didn't care. I wanted them out of my mouth at any cost. I figured that getting rid of them should put out the fire, but no such luck. What could I do to extinguish this fire in my mouth? I looked around the cage and started jumping from perch to perch. I opened my beak wide to let in some cool air, but this only made things worse. Then I noticed the water dish on the bottom of the cage. Water! That was the solution! Water puts out fires!

Superman would have been proud of me as I jumped to the bottom of the cage. I immediately leaped for my water dish. Thank goodness Jimmy had filled it with fresh water. If the vodka was still in there, my beak might have exploded. I put my mouth into the dish and started to drink. This worked like a charm. The fire was soon extinguished, so I thought. For some reason, a few seconds after I stopped drinking, the fire continued to rage on. So I continued to put my beak into the water. As a matter of fact, I decided to dunk my whole head into the water to get relief. There I was, a distinguished Macaw Parrot, bobbing for apples in a dish of water, except I had no apples. I must have looked ridiculous!

After carrying on in this way for a considerable amount of time, I noticed Beastly take the "pepper" from my cage and slip it into his pocket. The next thing I knew, he started shouting to the family saying that I had gone crazy. The entire family came running from all parts of the house. "The bird is going nuts! The bird is going nuts!", shouted Beastly. "He's dunkin' his head into the water dish. He's dunkin' his head into the water dish!"

The family watched in amazement as I continued to dunk my head into the water dish. My mouth was still on fire and the only way to get any relief was to cool it down in this way. "What a weird bird," said Beastly with a puzzled sort of look on his face. He acted as innocent as a newborn baby. Jimmy was becoming very upset as he watched me continue to dunk my head. But after awhile, I did manage to finally put out the flames. The fire was extinguished. My mouth was starting to return to normal. As I raised my head, I noticed the family staring at me. "Why were you dunkin' your head, you dopey bird?" asked Beastly, as if he didn't already know. He was like a vulture, circling around my cage, and I couldn't do anything about it.

Now the pieces of the puzzle started to come together, Beastly had pulled off a scheme and had gotten away with it. He was rather proud of himself and started prancing around like a peacock - strutting back and forth in front of my cage. Those pepper seeds were hot, and he knew it. Boy, was he gloating. I felt like a fool, trusting him in the first place. I glared at him. I gave him such a look that, if looks could kill, he would be dead more than twenty times. I now knew that he was perfectly aware of what he had done. From that point on, I made up my mind never to trust him again. Getting even with him would be something I was going to look forward to. I think he knew what I was thinking, so he started making fun of what had happened again and again. He kept repeating, "That dumb bird is dunkin' his head. That dumb bird is dunkin' his head", over and over. His mom told him to shut his mouth, but did he listen? Not Beastly! He kept chanting and chanting, "Dunkin', Dunkin', Dunkin' his head. Dunkin', Dunkin'

27

Dunkin' his head!"   Well, to make a long
story short, from that point on I had a
name.   Can you guess what name stuck with
me?   The name was Duncan.   I guess there
are worse names in the world for a parrot,
but all in all, the name Duncan isn't really
that bad.   As a matter of fact, it has sort
of a royal ring to it.   It sounds intelligent,
powerful, and sophisticated.   And just think,
I owe it all to my friend, Beastly!

CHAPTER 9

The next few days went real well for me. Everything calmed down, and I really got to know Jimmy. He paid a great deal of attention to me, and even tried to teach me how to talk. Talking was sort of a new experience for me. I knew how to chatter, scream, and squawk, but forming the letters of words presented some difficulty. Jimmy was patient, however, and worked with me night and day. By the end of the week I was able to say a few choice words like: "Hello", "Pretty Polly", "I Love You", and of course "Duncan". As a matter of fact, once I got the hang of it, talking was really very easy. All I had to do was repeat the words I heard around the house. I was even able to make sounds of different animals, if I wanted to - not bad for a rookie parrot.

The members of the family loved it when I said "Hello" to them as they entered the room. I called everyone by his proper name. I would call: "Hello, Mom", "Hello, Dad", "Hello, Jimmy", and, of course, "Hello, Beastly." That was one of my favorites. I learned it all by myself. Mom and Dad didn't even seem to mind that I called him by that name (probably because they thought he was a little stinker, and he probably deserved it anyway). It was great saying, "Hello, Beastly," to him when he came into the room. I especially loved to say it when he had a friend visiting him. However, it would take a lot more than a few "Hello, Beastlys" to get even with him for what he had already done to me.

One day, I remember saying, "Hello, Beastly," to him as he walked through the living room. The family was around, so he couldn't really smack my cage or do anything else nasty like that. So I continued to say, "Hello, Beastly,"over and over again. I would continue until he said, "Hello, Duncan," back to me. I would do that to all the members of the family. I'd say, "Hello, Jimmy," and he would say, "Hello," back to me. It was certainly a simple procedure, but Beastly refused to respond to my simple "Hello". I kept on him and continued to say, "Hello, Beastly." I knew it was bothering him, and I loved every minute of it. Well, he walked up to my cage and stared right at me. He said, "My name is Marvin. Say it. Marvin!" I turned my head and looked at him in a puzzled sort of way. I repeated, "Marvin." He was so happy with what I had said. "That's a good bird. Marvin. Say Marvin," he continued. I looked at him again and said, "Marvin." He was really pleased with himself when I said, "Hello, Marvin." As he started to walk from my cage he felt so proud of himself. He made a comment to the rest of the family about how he outsmarted that dumb bird. I couldn't let him get away with that, so before he left

the room I let out a beautiful, "Goodbye,
Beastly!" That made everyone in the family
laugh hysterically at him. He turned red
and left the room. This was only the
beginning of my "getting even" with Beastly.

CHAPTER 10

The holiday season was soon over and the kids had to go back to school. Because I was a parrot, I couldn't go with them, so I had to sit in my cage day after day. It was really boring. There was nothing for me to do. Luckily, Mom didn't work; at least, she didn't leave the house to work. She took care of a little two-year old boy during the day. His name was Billy. The kid was sort of neat. His mother would drop him off at the house every weekday morning and pick him up sometime before supper. I had no problem with this kid. As a matter of fact, we enjoyed each other's company.

Mom would sometimes sit him in front of the television. Little Billy loved cartoons. He would giggle and laugh at the silly animals running around the screen. I also was quite interested in the television. It was amazing to see these nasty little creatures punch, bite, and shoot each other. This television was full of such violence, but this little kid loved every minute of it. There was one program, however, that I loved to watch. It was on Public Television. It was called Sesame Street. I would listen to the little kid clap his hands and sing the theme song of the show. The show was on so often, that I even knew the theme song by heart. You could hear me singing,

"Sunny day, keeping the clouds away," most of the morning. Every once in a while the two year old and I would sing a duet together. Can you imagine how that must have sounded?

My most favorite character on the show was Big Bird. Who else could it be? I'm sure you've heard the expression, "Birds of a feather, stick together". Well, I just loved Big Bird. He was my hero. I would do anything for Big Bird. When he counted to ten, so did I. When he read a story, I listened closely. And when he taught us how to read, I paid careful attention. Big Bird was my inspiration; a great bird of the world. I would try to live up to his expectations of me. I would make him proud that I, too, was a bird.

It wasn't long before I was able to read some of the letters and words on the television screen. After a while, I could also add a few simple numbers. It was amazing what I could do if I really put my mind to it. But how would I be able to apply this knowledge to being a bird. I was cooped up in this cage. I should be let out and become a bird of the world. But, I figured, I was still young, so I put off my worldly ventures for another day.

My Sesame Street partner was a nice kid, but had a slight problem; he hadn't yet been potty-trained and always had a dirty diaper. The house would smell when this problem occurred, and even the cat would leave the room. I was confined to my cage, and therefore, was destined to stick it out with the little stinker. Sometimes Mom would come into the room just in time and take care of things, but, most of the time, she would be out of the room. It might be as long as fifteen minutes before she would realize a "dirty deed" had been done!

Now, being an intelligent bird, I figured out a quick way of getting Mom's attention. I would shout at the top of my lungs, "Billy did potty! Billy did potty!" This would bring her quickly into the room, remove the culprit, and dispose of the evidence. We had it down to a science; let's face it, when the going gets tough, the tough get going! Like Big Bird says, "Air pollution is harmful to nature, and it is our duty to try to prevent it. Fresh air is important to all forms of life, even a bird." So like a good friend of Big Bird, I am helping make the world a cleaner, fresher, and less smelly place to live. I may be a bird, but I'm no dope.

CHAPTER 11

As I grew, I was allowed more freedom around the house. Jimmy would take me out of my cage everyday after school and let me sit on his shoulder. I was too big for his finger by now, and it made me feel important sitting high up in the world. Jimmy would walk around the house while I hung on to him. Sometimes I would nibble on his ear and he would chuckle. Other times he would bring me to the refrigerator and we would "pig out" on snacks. We had a great time together. Jimmy would even let me sit on top of the table while he did his homework. I was able to read some of his papers, and he seemed to be a pretty bright boy. On the other hand, his brother, you know who, was no genius. This character couldn't spell to save his life, and his handwriting was terrible. He should have paid closer attention to Big Bird when he was younger.

I got to the point with Jimmy that when he came into the room after school, we would exchange greetings. Then I would say, "Duncan wants out - Duncan wants out." He would then open my door and I would hop onto his shoulder. We really had a great relationship. I had nothing to fear while I was with him. But when he wasn't around, well, that's another story.

I still hadn't figured out the "Ralph" story yet. But I had a suspicion the large gray cat, over on the other side of the room, had something to do with it. I never really trusted that cat from the first day I entered the house. It never really ever did anything to me, but there was something about the way it stared at my every move. It was a comfort being in the cage when that cat was around, and I always remembered what my father had said about cats.

One weekend afternoon the family decided to go out for awhile. This would be the first time I would be left home alone with no one in the house. I was alone at night when everyone went to sleep upstairs, and there was no problem then, so this should not be any different - should it? Well, I was entirely wrong. As soon as the front door locked, that lazy old cat went on the prowl. It walked right straight up to my cage and proceeded to watch my every move. As I rocked on my swing, the cat's head rocked back and forth. Not only did his head rock, but his tail did also. Why did this cat all of a sudden show an interest in me? Maybe he wanted to become my friend, or maybe he was curious. Whatever it was, I didn't like it.

There was really nothing I could do about the cat at this point, so I decided to go on with my everyday boring bird activities. There was nothing better to do, so I decided to sing a song. There I was, swinging on my swing without a care in the world, except for that feline under me watching my every move. Since my favorite song in the whole world was the Sesame Street song, I decided to sing it again and again. Big Bird was truly an inspiration in my life.

I suspected that the cat was getting restless while looking at me. He started to pace, back and forth, in front of my cage. What was this character up to, anyway? I wasn't bothering him. Nobody ever bothered him. As a matter of fact, the cat was the only one in the family that did as he pleased. Nobody could make him do anything. As far as I was concerned, this cat was a worthless member of the family. I had more respect for Beastly because at least Beastly was dumb enough to get himself into trouble and would always get caught by his parents. This cat, on the other hand, never did anything wrong, or, at least, never got caught in the act. Maybe Ralph had an answer or two about that.

By now, the cat was circling my cage. I had the feeling he wanted to attack, but I had nothing to fear since I was protected by bars and hanging from the ceiling by a large hook. So I figured, "Go for it, Cat. Give it your best shot." Suddenly, there was a huge shadow covering my cage. Had the sun finally gone down? Was there a solar eclipse taking place? Not really. That cat had decided to leap onto my cage and hold on for dear life. He looked ridiculous holding on to my cage with all four of his legs stretched around the bars. He couldn't do anything since I was protected, so he tried hissing and spitting at me. What was he trying to do? Did he think I was stupid enough to stick my head through the bars into his mouth? What did I look like, a Dodo Bird? As far as I was concerned, the Dodo was on the outside of the cage, not on the inside.

Well, it started becoming annoying having this stupid cat hugging my cage. Why didn't it just let go? It knew it couldn't get me. And why was it making all of that unnecessary noise? At this point, I felt I had to improve on the situation and make the cat let go of my home. I said a few phrases to persuade this wonderful kitty to leave me alone. I tried, "Get off - Get down - Stop it - Leave me alone - No - Bad Boy - I'll tell Mom." Now all of these used to work on Beastly, but why wasn't this stupid cat listening to me. I knew the cat had to be smarter than Beastly. Everyone was smarter than Beastly.

The cat had no intention of stopping his nonsense, so, I figured, it was time for a plan. I looked around the inside of the cage and noticed that the tip of the cat's tail was sticking in between the bars. "Aha!

That gives me an idea," I thought. I jumped to the bottom of the cage and grabbed the tail. Now, did I bite it? No, not me. Did I pull it? No, not me. I handled it ever so gently and tied it into a knot around one of my perches. I learned that from watching Sesame Street. It was difficult, but by using my beak and feet I was able to do it. The stupid cat had no idea what I was doing, because it was still hissing and carrying on. Now, what could I do to correct this situation? Here I was, a peaceful bird, minding my own business in my cage, and this nasty cat starts to mess around with me. Being a polite bird, I asked him to stop. He didn't listen, so I tied his tail to the perch of my cage. He still wouldn't stop annoying me, so what should I do? I did what any other bird would do in my situation. I opened my mouth as wide as I could, and bit his tail. That sure got his attention! As a matter of fact, it not only got his attention, but it also made him let go of the cage. Now, I was in luck, the cat was no longer wrapped around my cage. There was sunlight coming through from all sides now. But there was still something wrong - the Poor Kitty wasn't anywhere to be found. I looked all around the room for him, but he seemed to have disappeared. The Poor Kitty must have run away, or maybe it was hanging around someplace else.

It was interesting when the family returned home. The first words out of

Mom's mouth were, "Oh, my goodness!" Dad said, "What in the world?" Jimmy shouted, "Bad cat!" Beastly was amused by the whole situation and said, "Way to go, Duncan!" Now what could they be talking about? They weren't here for any of the action. I guess the evidence that was hanging around painted a perfect picture for them. What evidence am I talking about? Well, remember I tied the cat's tail to my perch? Well, it was still tied, and Poor Kitty was hanging around under my cage the whole time. He was helpless and couldn't move. A low moan came from his mouth as he hung there.

I guess I showed that cat that he shouldn't mess around with me. He didn't bother me anymore after that. As a matter of fact, he was a little nervous when I was out of my cage. Sometimes, while I was on Jimmy's shoulder, I would raise my wings when I knew the cat was looking at me. This made him jump up and leave the room immediately. That cat actually turned out to be a big chicken.

And as for Ralph, the mystery of his disappearance was solved. I heard Dad mention that I was a smart, tough bird. He knew I could handle myself in any difficult situation. I'm sure he was speaking about the "Hanging Kitty" incident. Even Beastly made a remark that I wouldn't wind up being "Cat Food" like Ralph was. Poor Ralph must have been an unfortunate victim of the cat.

I'm thankful I didn't wind up like him. I guess some of us have it, and some of us don't. I happened to be one of the lucky ones.

CHAPTER 12

One day, after school, Jimmy came running into the house. It was report card day. From what I understood, a report card was a list of letters given to students showing how well they did in school. The letters ranged from A to F. I knew my letters, thanks to Big Bird, so I was sure that Jimmy would get the highest letters there were. As he took me out of the cage, I noticed his report card, and I was correct about his letters. There were mostly A's and a few B's. He was very proud of it because he had worked very hard everyday after school doing homework and studying for tests. We sat at the table, along with his mom, and admired his report card. Jimmy was very proud of himself, and so was I. After all, I would help him with his work at night.

Well, there was one member of the family that was not looking forward to showing his report card to his parents. Can you guess who that was? I watched my old friend, Beastly, walk quietly into the house that same day. He was looking around and acting very suspicious. He reached into a book that he was carrying and took out a card similar to the one Jimmy brought home. Then he stretched his arm as high as he could, and placed the card on a high ledge above my cage. "This was pretty strange-even for Beastly," I thought to myself. I didn't pay anymore attention to him after that, and decided to take a short nap.

At dinner that evening, Mom was telling Dad about Jimmy's report card, and how well he had done. Then Dad asked Beastly where his report card was. Beastly played dumb and said that it would be coming out next week. He insisted that his school was a little behind in its paperwork and there was no need to worry. Mom seemed concerned because everyone always got their report cards on the same day. It had always been done that way. But being a trusting individual, she told him to make sure he would let her see the report card as soon as he got it. I was listening to this conversation, and being suspicious of Beastly, I decided to do a little detective work.

Once dinner was over, I called to Jimmy, "Duncan wants out. Duncan wants out." My friend walked over to my cage, opened the door, and let me walk onto his shoulder. Now, from his shoulder I jumped onto the top of my cage. Then I said, "Duncan stay here. Duncan stay here." Jimmy understood what I wanted and allowed me to stand on top of my cage. This was the first step in my investigation - to find out what was on that card Beastly had hidden.

Beastly thought he had pulled off another caper. He was so proud of himself that he went upstairs to his room to gloat about it. I, on the other hand, knew he was up to something. I was able to see the card from where I was standing. All I had to do was jump from the top of my cage to the ledge. I made sure no one was looking at me when I did this. After all, a detective can't let anyone know what he is doing. Everything must be done in secret. Sherlock Holmes would have been pleased with my quick leap. I grabbed the card in my beak. and quickly jumped back to the top of my cage. No one noticed a thing. I opened up the card with my beak and stood on top of it with my feet. I started to read it and found out that Beastly had lied. This was his report card. I couldn't read all the words on it, but I was sure about it. The report card wasn't like Jimmy's, it was terrible, Beastly got three D's and two F's. Boy, was this report card a stinker! No wonder he tried to hide it from his parents.

Now that I had solved the case, what should I do? Should I mind my own business, or should I expose the criminal. It didn't take me very long to figure out that this was the perfect opportunity to get even with Beastly. So I started to think of a good plan. The "Water" and "Pepper Seed" incidents were still fresh in my mind. Let's face it - a bird has to do, what a bird has to do.

If my plan was going to work, I needed everyone to come into the room - even Beastly. I had to see the look on his face when he got caught. My plan was simple- I would act real cute and say a few things the family had never heard before. They loved when I put on a show for them because I was such a little ham. I then started speaking, "I know a secret. I know a secret. Beastly is bad. Beastly is bad. I know something you don't know. I know something you don't know." This immediately got everyone's attention. Mom called Beastly down from his room to see what was happening. I carried on and on and waited for the stage to be set. Finally when everyone was in the room, I was ready to expose the criminal. I remembered this from watching the television: Sherlock Holmes would always bring everyone into the room when he was ready to solve the case. In this case, however, the butler didn't do it, it was Beastly.

All eyes were upon me. The stage had been set. I was ready to name the culprit. I stuck out my feathers, perked up my head, and started to shout, "Beastly got two F's. Beastly got two F's!" Everyone looked at him with puzzled expressions. "Shut up, you stupid bird!" screamed Beastly. "What are you talking about?" He then walked toward my cage and took a swat at me, but missed. At this point I picked up the report card with my beak and dropped it to the floor.

Beastly tried to step on it to cover it with his foot, but Dad grabbed him by the ear and pulled him back. Mom picked up the report card and proceeded to read it. She was shaking her head back and forth. She gave the card to Dad and he, too, shook his head. Mom, Dad, and Beastly left the room, went into the kitchen, and closed the door. Even though the door was closed, I could still hear all the shouting and screaming. Beastly was finally caught red-handed. He was nailed by me - Ace Detective - Duncan, the Parrot.

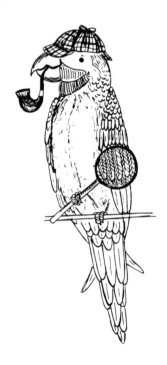

CHAPTER 13

Spring was upon us, and all of nature was in bloom. The smell of flowers filled the day as a warm breeze blew in from outdoors. I was officially one year old, and I was also fully grown. Mother Nature had been good to me because I not only was a pretty young bird, but I became a beautiful adult parrot. If only my parents could see me now. They would be very pleased with the way I turned out.

I didn't see as much of Jimmy as I did in the past. He had lots of friends, and many things to do outside, now that the weather was warmer. I felt lonely and missed him, but tried to entertain myself. Dad built me a perch that I was allowed to stand on when I wasn't in my cage. The cage was a little snug for me because I had grown so much, and the perch was a way for me to get exercise and stretch my legs. Jimmy would put me on the perch when he left for school in the morning, and leave my cage open, in case I needed to eat or drink anything during the day.

On the weekends Jimmy would take me outside with him in the backyard. I loved it out there. The air was fresh and there were many different sights to see. I could have flown away and gone out into the world on my own, but I didn't. I had a great life here, and I wouldn't trade that for anything. However, I did fly around in the backyard occasionally, just to get the feeling of being a real parrot. I would fly from branch to branch in a nearby tree. But when Jimmy called me back to the house, I would return immediately. Sometimes he would leave me in the yard by myself. I would sun myself and preen my feathers in the sunshine. The cat would also be outdoors when the weather was nice. I would watch it prowl around the yard looking for little birds or mice. It was peculiar watching the cat. He would sneak up behind some small animal, wait silently, and spring on top of it. He almost always caught his prey, and then started to play with it. One thing he never did, however, was to mess with me. I'm sure that cat still remembers the day we "Hung Around" my cage together.

One day, while I was flying from branch to branch, I spied a small area of ground in the yard below. I floated softly to that spot, and saw that it was a grave. On top of the grave was a marker which said, "HERE LIES RALPH, A FRIEND OF JIMMY. TAKEN IN THE PRIME OF HIS LIFE. LOVED BY ALL. REST IN PEACE." What a sad thought to know that my predecessor ended up here. I glared at the cat across the yard and started flapping my wings wildly. The cat, who had a tiny mouse in his mouth, immediately dropped it and ran into the house. I made a decision,

48

from that day on: to protect the animals in the yard from that cruel killer. This I would do in memory of Ralph.

Our cat wasn't the only problem in the yard in this neighborhood. Other cats would patrol the yards looking for some sort of sport. I would look forward to them coming. I had ways of dealing with cats - ways that only a parrot could appreciate. I remember one cat who was looking for a little excitement. He was bothering the little birds in the birdbath in the middle of our yard. He would sneak into the yard by pressing a loose fence board. The board shut like a gate. Once inside the yard, he would terrorize the area. He would sneak up on the birds in the birdbath and try to grab them. Now, cats don't like water, and I knew it. I would watch this one stand on the edge of the birdbath balancing itself so it wouldn't get wet. I think the other birds knew this stupid cat couldn't get them because it wouldn't go near the water, so they kept just far enough out of reach. What a stupid cat. It was actually afraid to get its feet wet. I now had the perfect opportunity to teach this cat a lesson. The next day as I watched him enter the yard, I waited for him to climb the birdbath. Once on top, he did his thing - being very careful not to get his feet wet. This time, however, he seemed more daring. He leaned over a little more than usual trying to snatch his prey from the water. When I saw this, I sprang into action. I flew straight toward the cat from behind. I quickly let out a piercing shriek that scared the poor feline. He immediately lost his balance and fell straight into the water. Poor Kitty was all wet. He also had his first swimming lesson. It was hysterical watching the cat run through the yard shaking water from all parts of its body.

Another cat even had the nerve to try and catch me. This one would come from another opening in the fence and try to sneak up behind me. I would let him get real close. When he jumped for me, I jumped from my perch, and the cat would land flat on his face.

The best experience I had with a cat was when I let it chase me up a tree. I would flutter, just out of its reach, so that it would continue to climb after me. The stupid cat didn't realize how high it was climbing. All it wanted to do was to get me. Higher and higher we went. Finally, when we got to the top of the tree, it dawned on the Dumb Kitty that he had climbed too high. I was able to flutter down back to my perch, and was entertained for the rest of the day. The cat was too scared to move; all it did was sit and cry. It turned around, and around looking for a way to get down. It finally took a call to the Fire Department to get him down from the tree. After that, the cats must have put

out the word: Duncan's backyard is off
limits to all cats!

CHAPTER 14

I might appear to be a troublemaker picking on cats, but I am really a very nice, well behaved bird. I always do as I am told, and never bother anyone who doesn't deserve it. Now, the cats in the neighborhood deserved everything they got. My arch enemy, Beastly, also deserved everything he got. However, since the report card incident, I really hadn't any reason to bother him. He was behaving very well, and he was even doing much better in school. He even acted almost like a human being in front of his parents. I was really impressed on how he had matured. He was extra nice to me too. He was always very polite, and he never even as much as banged my cage as he had done in the past. Was something wrong with Beastly? Was he alright, or was he planning revenge on me? I guess only time would tell.

Another beautiful weekend was upon us, and as usual, I was brought outside to stand guard and protect the little creatures of my domain. I patrolled the yard like "ROBO PARROT", part robot and part parrot, whose purpose in life was to stop crime. "Robo Parrot", I liked the sound of that, and I tried to live up to my name. While performing my patrol duty this weekend, I noticed that Beastly had wandered outside and sat on a lounge chair right next to me. He had a book with him. This didn't bother me. After all, it was his yard too, but the thing that shocked me is that good, old Beastly actually started to read this book. I was once again impressed. Beastly had come a long way since our last encounter. I almost felt proud to be a member of his family, but I'm sure that was only a temporary feeling. Somehow Beastly would probably be back to normal in a few weeks or so.

Since there was no action going on in the yard, I declared the grounds to be secure, and decided to take a nap. There was nothing like napping in the warm outdoors. I must have really been sleeping soundly, because when I awoke, I noticed that my leg had a long string tied around it. I wondered where it came from and how it got there, but then I remembered who was sitting next to me. Good old, Beastly was at it again. What could he be up to now? I tried to untie the string, but it wouldn't budge. I turned my head to look at Beastly and he was smiling a real nasty smile. Oh, Boy, now what was in store for me? I didn't want to hang around and find out, so I took off like a jet heading towards the trees. This was exactly what Beastly wanted me to do. When the string ran out, he pulled me right down to the ground. I fell with a loud thud. I stood up in a sort of puzzled way, not knowing what had happened to me, and, like a dope, I took off again. I've done some pretty stupid things in my time, but this had to be on top of the pile. Guess what happened when I ran out of string again? Beastly pulled, and I came down. The next thing the Boy Wonder did was to pretend to be a cowboy. He took the string and started to twirl it around his head. Guess who was at the other end of the string, over his head, and spinning like a top? If you haven't guessed by now - it was me. What a terrible feeling it was! I had no control over what was happening to me. Around, and around, and around I'd go - where I'd stop, nobody would know, except, maybe, for Beastly.

Soon afterwards, I must have passed out, because when I awoke there was no string around my leg, there was no Beastly, and I was lying alone on the grass in the middle of the yard. I tried to get on my feet, and when I did, I started to walk around in circles. Was I ever dizzy. No matter where I tried to walk, I couldn't get there, I just kept walking in circles. I figured, this is no way for a bird to behave, so I decided to fly back to the safety of my perch. This turned out to be worse than walking. Even though I tried to fly back to my perch, I flew straight into a tree. Bang! The sound echoed through the yard. My beak felt as though it had been bent in half. There I was, lying in a heap on the ground, with my feathers sticking out all over the place. I must have looked like a jet that just crashed into the side of a mountain.

Once the dizziness wore off, I was able to make my way back to the safety of my perch. Then I noticed Beastly standing in the doorway of the house, laughing and laughing. Once again, he had done it to me. Well, tomorrow was another day, Beastly, I had all night to work on my revenge.

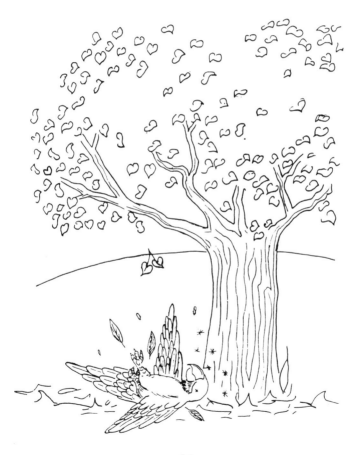

CHAPTER 15

Sunday was just as beautiful a day as Saturday. My feathered friends were singing sweetly from the branches of their trees, and the bees were busy buzzing from flower to flower collecting nectar to make honey. I was especially alert today after the episode I had with Beastly yesterday. I promised myself I would get even with him for turning me into a miniature satellite and spinning me around his head. But that was yesterday, and today was a new day. I would spend this day GETTING EVEN WITH BEASTLY!

Like nothing had happened, Beastly came out of the house, again with his book, and parked himself in the same chair as yesterday. I looked at him, and he looked at me. We both ignored each other. I think we got along best when we did that. Beastly proceeded to read again, and I started patrolling the backyard for any potential crime wave. When I had finished, I noticed that this time Beastly was the one who had fallen asleep. Now was the time for me to carry out my revenge. I had spent almost the entire night planning it, so I had to act quickly before he woke up. I had several ideas of what I could do to him, but something I saw under his chair changed my strategy. Under Beastly's chair was an anthill. Perhaps I could persuade these little insect friends to pay Beastly a visit. The first thing I thought about was how to attract the ants. I knew ants liked sweet things, because I learned that on Sesame Street. But where could I get something sweet? Again, I noticed bees on the flowers. Nectar. I'll use nectar to attract the ants. Nectar is sweet. But how could I get the nectar to Beastly? I thought and thought. Then I decided to take a thin tree branch and rub it through the tops of the flowers. I figured that the bees wouldn't mind sharing a little bit of nectar with me, so I found a thin branch and was on my way.

When this was finished, I leaned the branch from the anthill to Beastly's chair. I also found a piece of candy laying on the ground. The sun was starting to warm it up, and it was very sticky. I put this sweet treasure at the top of the stick, which formed a little highway to Beastly's pants. I forgot to mention that the candy would be able to fall into the seat of Beastly's pants when he moved suddenly. You see, his shirt was up just enough for me to stick it there. But I can't think of any reason why Beastly would move suddenly, can you?

Well, the plan started to come together. The ants were parading up the branch just like I had planned. They went right for the sticky candy. More and more ants came to get a piece of the action. There were so many ants on the candy now, that you couldn't see it at all. It disappeared into a swarm of ants. It looked like an antball. Well, needless to say, Beastly moved when he felt something crawling on his body. He moved perfectly. The antball slipped under the belt of his pants, and the rest was history.

I never saw anyone move as fast as Beastly. He jumped out of his chair like a rocket and moved around the yard, smacking his back and backside, but all of this movement caused the antball to move farther down his pants. I couldn't help but laugh, seeing Beastly slap and scratch. He just couldn't control the ants. All of a sudden, he unloosened his belt and pulled off his pants. He looked so silly running around the yard in his underwear. I'll never forget that comical scene of Beastly in the backyard in his underwear.

Mom came outside when she heard all the commotion. Even Jimmy, who was next door at a friend's house, came running when he heard the racket. The little girls who lived behind us peeked over the fence to see what was going on. Can you imagine the picture of Beastly running around in his underwear in the back yard screaming and scratching like a wildman? The little girls giggled at him, Mom started chasing him and slapping the ants off with her broom, and Jimmy walked up to me and said, "Duncan,

you bad bird," and winked at me as he
smiled.

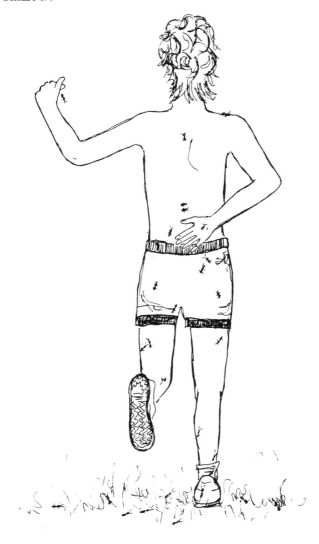

CHAPTER 16

The person in the family I probably spent the least amount of time with was Dad. A good reason for this is because he worked during the day, and was out of town on business a lot. However, we did spend a few evenings a week together reading the newspaper. After dinner, he would go to his easy chair with the paper and begin to read. I was always on my perch, waiting for him to begin. I would jump from my perch to the headrest of his chair and read along with him. He didn't seem to mind me reading over his shoulder. I'm sure he thought I was just looking at the pictures. Really, what parrot can read? If he only knew what was going on in that little bird brain of mine.

One evening, there was a headline that read, "CAT BURGLAR STRIKES AGAIN." What was this? A person breaking into houses and stealing cats? I couldn't believe anyone would want to do that. Steal a parrot, a dog, or even a mouse, but a cat? As far as I was concerned, cats were worthless. I had experience with our house cat, and believe me, he wasn't worth two cents. All he did all day long was sleep, eat, scratch the furniture, cough up fur balls, chase animals in the yard, and make a mess around his litter box. I guess some people are strange, but if stealing cats makes them happy, who am I to judge them?

Dad mentioned to Mom that the Cat Burglar broke into two houses down the street yesterday. He was concerned that our house might be next. Mom assured him that we would have no problem with a Cat Burglar because we were protected by ROBO PARROT. She would call me that because of the way I would keep a close eye on the backyard to keep out all intruders. She then came over to where I was standing and started to stroke my feathers. She looked at me and said, "If anyone tries to break into the house, I'm sure Duncan will let out a few screams and scare him away." She was right. I could do that. I was tough, and I was smart. I would scare anyone away that was trying to break into our house. If a Cat Burglar tried to steal our cat, I would most certainly stop him. I thought for a moment, and realized what I was saying. Thinking about it, would I really want to stop a Cat Burglar from stealing our Precious Kitty? I thought and thought. It didn't take very long to realize that I didn't care in the least if Kitty was stolen. As far as I was concerned, I would try to help the Cat Burglar do it. Any bird in my position would do the same, wouldn't he?

CHAPTER 17

That evening, after the family went to bed, I was excited about the thought of meeting the Cat Burglar. There was no way I was going to try to stop him from doing his job. If he wanted to steal our Kitty, he could have him. I would keep as silent as a mouse. I made up my mind not to interfere in the slightest. After all, one hand washes the other. He was doing me a favor by taking our cat, and I was doing him a favor by not stopping him. That seemed fair to me.

A few hours later, just as I had expected, I heard a slight noise at the front door. It sounded as though someone was playing with the lock. I heard this click, and in walked a man dressed entirely in black. He proceeded to walk through the room shining a flashlight from place to place. As he searched the house with his light, I wanted to tell him, right out, where the cat was. I felt like shouting at the top of my lungs, but I controlled myself. I figured that this man was a professional, and he knew his job. He would find the cat sooner or later. My guess was right, but instead of finding the cat while searching with the flashlight, he stepped on its tail. The cat gave off a sharp scream. To my surprise, the Cat Burglar kicked the cat and said, "Get out of my way, you stupid cat!"

I was confused. If the Cat Burglar came into the house to steal our cat, why was he telling it to get out of his way?

I continued to watch him walk around the room. He proceeded to take out a large black bag about the size of a pillowcase. I figured he was going to put the cat into this bag. Well, I was wrong. Instead, he started to take other things from the house. He took Mom's silver candlesticks, Dad's watch, and even a few things from Mom's china closet. Now the pieces of the puzzle were starting to come together. A Cat Burglar doesn't steal cats. The reason they must be called Cat Burglars is because they are sneaky - like cats. Right then, I made up my mind to teach this guy a lesson. How could he possibly think he could get away with stealing valuables from our house with ROBO PARROT around. As he walked from room to room, I waited until he was finished with his work. I gave him this extra time, because I knew that outside the house the policemen were patrolling the neighborhood in police cars. Every few minutes a police car would come past the house. There was one at the end of the street now, because I could see the headlights of the car. It would be in front of our house in a matter of seconds.

When everything was ready, I shouted at the top of my lungs, "THIS IS THE POLICE. WE KNOW YOU ARE IN THERE.

THE HOUSE IS SURROUNDED. COME OUT WITH YOUR HANDS UP!" The Cat Burglar didn't know what to do. He saw the police car outside, and figured they knew he was in the house. He then opened our front door and shouted to the police, "DON'T SHOOT, I GIVE UP!" The policemen heard someone shouting at them and stopped the car to see what was going on. When they saw the Cat Burglar with his hands over his head, and carrying the bag of loot, they figured he was surrendering to them.

By now, my family was awake and already downstairs. They were able to see the Cat Burglar being arrested by the police. Dad couldn't understand how the policemen had caught him. Then he looked at me. I had a gleam in my eye. He said, "I guess watching those police movies on television has paid off, hasn't it, Duncan?" He winked at me and went outside to talk to the policemen. Mom was quite impressed with the way I had handled the whole situation. She said, "Well, ROBO PARROT, it looks like you wrapped up another case," and she was right. Things might not have turned out exactly the way I wanted, but I had livened up the evening a bit.

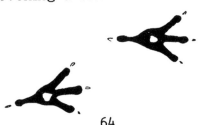

CHAPTER 18

One night, while I was watching Jimmy do his homework, he showed me a picture of a beautiful bird. This bird was, by far, the most beautiful bird in the world. Naturally, I was looking at a picture of a Macaw Parrot. He said that his class was studying South America this month. It was interesting to see some of the animals I grew up with in the pet store right in front of me. There was a picture of Cousin Toucan; Bobo, the spider monkey; and lots of others. I felt sort of homesick for the pet store. After all, it was there that I experienced my first breath of life, even if the pet store air wasn't that fresh.

Jimmy told me that he had to do a report on South America. He said it had to be special, because he wanted to get an "A". Upon hearing this, I realized that it was my time to get out and see the world. Maybe Jimmy could use me in his report. I quickly said, "Let Duncan help! Let Duncan help!" He thought it was a good idea and started thinking about how I could be used in his project. I was more than happy to help Jimmy, but my intentions were not truly honorable. I figured that if I helped him, he would have to take me to school with him. School was always somewhere I wanted to go. The idea must have been put into my brain by Big Bird when I was younger. Now my wish had finally come true.

Jimmy thought about how he was going to use me in his project, and decided to make it simple. He would ask me some important questions, and I would give the correct answers. That sounded simple enough. We couldn't miss the "A". It was a great idea. What could be better than having a parrot from South America answer questions about its homeland.

The report took about a week of preparation. I had to study the answers carefully. There were basic questions about South America, which included mountains, rivers, animals, and lakes. We were just about set for our presentation to his teacher and class. I was on my first road to seeing the outside world.

Jimmy worked out the details with the school and decided that Friday would be the best day to bring me into his classroom. Friday happened to be a half day. The teacher figured the excitement might be too much for me sitting in a class for a full day. He didn't know me very well, did he? Friday was two days away, and I was as jumpy as a grasshopper. I couldn't wait to finally get my beak into a book at school. I would be the first one in my family to get an education. My parents would surely be proud of me. Who knows what this may

66

lead to - High School, College, Medical
School - the possibilities were endless.

CHAPTER 19

Being in school sounded great, in theory, but there was one problem with that, how was I going to get there? The school was several miles away, so Jimmy had to take a bus every day. The only way I would be able to get there was to take the school bus. I never imagined that I would someday ride on one of those ugly, yellow school buses. I often thought, "Why did they paint those things that disgusting color?" Maybe someone had a lot of extra yellow paint, or perhaps, this way the little kids wouldn't go on the wrong bus. I guess the best answer to that is so other drivers can tell it is a school bus and drive extra carefully, especially when a school bus driver is loading and unloading school children from the school bus. Whatever the reason for a school bus's color, I, Duncan the Parrot, was about to go onto one. It was Friday morning, and I was extra excited. Maybe Jimmy would let me sit next to the window. He told me kids usually fight over a window seat. Or, maybe we could sit in the back of the school bus. I hear that's where the cool kids sit. I was getting even more excited just thinking about it. But my mouth dropped open when Jimmy came to my perch with a box a little bigger than me. I looked at him and turned my head slightly. He knew what I was thinking and said, "Sorry, Duncan, this is the only way they will let me bring you on the bus. They have rules about pets." I think Jimmy was more upset than I was, but he had to follow the rules, as stupid as they were. How could they consider me, Duncan the Parrot, a common pet. I had a reputation around the neighborhood. Cats feared me, the police respected me; I was almost a living legend. But, legend or not, I had to climb into the box, and be carried onto the bus in order to go to school.

The walk to the bus stop was quite bumpy. Jimmy tried to carry me as carefully as he could. I trusted him, and I was sure he wouldn't drop me. Could you imagine what kind of a situation I would be in if Beastly was carrying me? Thank goodness he started school earlier that Jimmy. I really wasn't very comfortable, but if this is what I had to go through to get to school, I would do it. Remember, as I have always said, "A bird has to do what a bird has to do," and I always knew that it wasn't easy getting an education. I hoped the remainder of my day would be better. Actually, it couldn't have been worse.

CHAPTER 20

I was very uncomfortable in the tiny box. I couldn't open my wings to stretch, and I couldn't scratch an itch if I needed to. Why do all my new experiences have to start with me cramped in a tiny box? I remember when I was brought home from the pet shop, the same thing had happened to me there, too. Well, anyway, I was finally on the school bus on my way to school.

I had no idea where we were sitting, so I pretended that I was seated in the back of the bus with the cool kids. I mean, where else could I sit? I'm definitely cool. I heard Jimmy talking to some of his friends. Several of them asked what he had in the box. He tried to act innocent, and told them it was his lunch. They all accepted this answer except for one nasty little girl. She proceeded to ask him why his lunch box had holes in the top of it. Jimmy told her to mind her own business and leave him alone. I could tell that this girl was trouble, and I didn't even know her. At one point, she quickly grabbed the box away from Jimmy and started shaking it to see if it made any noise. The box made noise, alright. The box had screams coming out of it. The girl became startled and dropped the box onto the floor of the bus. One of the wise guys sitting in front of us decided to give the box a good kick. Another kid did the same thing. I was kicked up and down the aisle two times. Now I know what a hockey puck feels like getting knocked around the rink all day long.

The bus driver, who was a very large woman, saw what was happening and quickly pulled the bus over to the side of the road. "What's going on here?" she screamed. I could tell that she was angry, by the tone of her voice. Jimmy quickly stood up and went searching for me. He told the driver what had happened. By then I became excited and started to yell, "HELP - HELP!" A sweet little girl picked up my box and handed it to Jimmy. She felt embarrassed for the rest of the children. The driver demanded to see what was in the box, so Jimmy brought me up to her. She asked that the box be opened. Jimmy was concerned about the rules of no pets. The driver told him it was no problem, and to do it anyway. That's all I needed to hear. Once the box opened, I popped out my head. One hundred eyes stared at me. My feathers were a little ruffled, but I was fine. The driver petted me on the beak, and warned the children not to mess with her friend, the bird. If anyone did, they would have to answer to her. She also changed a few seats around and let Jimmy and me ride in the back of the bus. I felt as though things were starting to get better. The rest of the day would tell more.

CHAPTER 21

Riding in the back of the bus was great. I was able to look out of the window and watch the world go by. The kids on the bus were still shocked about me being there in the first place. Most of them just stared and stared. That nasty little girl who started the whole thing, started to inch her way to the back of the bus. She traveled slowly from seat to seat like a cat on the prowl. I knew there was a reason I didn't like this girl: she reminded me of a sneaky cat. Even her voice reminded me of a cat. I could tell we would not become friends. Actually, I owed her one for getting me kicked around. I would have plenty of time to do that later, but, for now, I was enjoying my ride.

The kids on the bus started asking Jimmy questions about me. He told them about the project. They were excited about having a real, live parrot on the bus. The kids in Jimmy's class were even more excited about me spending the day with them in the classroom. Things were certainly starting to go better. Jimmy had me say, "Hello, Bus Driver." She thought that was cute and told me that I could ride on her bus anytime. She turned out to be a very nice lady.

The bus slowly came to a stop and before I knew it, I was at school. It was a huge building with lots of windows. I was starting to get excited again. I kept saying, "School, school, Duncan likes school." One of the creeps that kicked my box before heard this and shouted out, "I figured he was a dumb bird. He even likes school." Some of the other kids laughed at his stupid joke. Jimmy felt embarrassed. The cute little girl who rescued me, told him to shut his mouth. Some of the other kids supported her. It felt good to have friends who liked me, but I realized that the world was no different from my own home. There were plenty of Beastlys to deal with on the outside world, even in school. I would have to deal with these kids at another time. My goal now was to get into that school with no problems, but I realized I had to do it by going into that tiny box again. The things a bird will do to get an education! Big Bird, this had better be worth it!

CHAPTER 22

Jimmy tucked me safely away into my box again. He thanked the bus driver for all of her help, and, before I knew it, we were on our way again. Surprisingly enough, we made it to the classroom without any problems. Jimmy's teacher was already in the classroom when we got there and instructed all the other students to take a seat. He then asked Jimmy to bring his box to the front of the room. At the same time, he told the class what was in the box and for them to stay in their seats.

My time had come. I was finally in school. The first sight I would see would be the inside of a classroom. I was getting excited again. Jimmy opened the box and I lifted up my head. I stood up and stretched my wings. The class responded with a low, "WOW!" Was I an impressive sight, or what? I bet Jimmy already had an "A" for his project, and I didn't do anything yet.

The teacher introduced me to the class. He said, "Boys and girls, this is Duncan. Please say hello to him." The class responded with, "Hello, Duncan." I was feeling good about the whole situation, so I decided to dazzle them a bit. I said, "Hello, Class. Hello, Teacher." Everyone, including the teacher was shocked. The teacher responded with, "My name is Mr. Morgan." I felt cute again, so I said, "Hello, Mr. Morgan." He was very impressed with me already. I could tell by the surprised look on his face. Jimmy told me to cool it for awhile and not to be a show-off. The class giggled when he said that.

Mr. Morgan was a fairly young teacher. He was tall and thin and wore dark framed glasses. He had a perch all ready for me in the front of the room. He was a very considerate person, I thought, looking after me like that. He then reminded the class that I would be used later, for Jimmy's project, and they should try to concentrate on their school work. The class gave a low moan, because they realized that the entire day would not be all fun and games.

Now, here I sat, on my perch in a classroom. I love it when a plan comes together. All I had to do was to listen and learn. School was surely going to be a place I most certainly would enjoy. Class didn't even start yet, and I loved it already. Did I have a good attitude, or what?

I looked around the classroom while Mr. Morgan was preparing to teach a lesson. I noticed books, maps, and plenty of paper. I wondered if I would be able to use any of that stuff today? In my inspection of the classroom, my eyes met with my old friend from the bus, the Cat Girl. She was staring at me, just like a cat. I wonder if she was thinking cat thoughts also? There was something about her that made me feel uneasy. I just couldn't put my beak on it yet, but I'm sure I would. Another familiar face in the crowd was the young gentleman from the bus that decided to play hockey with my box. I also remember him to be the "wise guy" who teased me about liking school. I'd been in school for almost ten minutes, and I'd already met a few Beastlys. I wondered if the world was full of Beastly-like people?

Mr. Morgan finally started the lesson. It was a science lesson on using the sun and a magnifying glass to make heat. My eyes were glued to him. My ears listened to his every word. I watched him call on some of the other students for answers to questions he had asked. Many responded with correct answers. Jimmy raised his hand for mostly every answer. I was very proud of him. There were two children, however, who didn't raise their hands to answer a single question. Even when the teacher tried to get them to answer, they didn't know it. These two kids could care less about school. Can you guess who they were? The girl's name was Kitty - can you believe that name? And guess who she was? That's right, my old friend from the bus, the Cat Girl. The other one's name was Marvin-That's Beastly's real name. He was the wise guy on the bus. Was that a coincidence, or does history have a way of repeating itself?

Of all the people in the world, these two bothersome kids were named after a cat and a Beastly. It was pretty funny when you thought about it.

I watched Kitty for a while. She was in her own little world. After a while, I couldn't bear to watch her any longer, because she had a disgusting habit. The habit was so disgusting that it made me turn my head. It would even make a cat turn its head. After seeing her do this, I would put her into one of the top ten gross-outs of all time. The horrible habit this girl had was to constantly pick her nose and wipe it under her desk. How gross! I felt like shouting to her to use a tissue. Even the kids around her were grossed-out. I watched them turn their heads in disgust. No matter how I tried to look away my eyes always seemed to watch her gross actions. Finally, I couldn't take it any more. She was distracting and annoying to me and the class, so I raised up my feathers and squawked, "KITTY IS PICKING HER NOSE-YUCK - KITTY IS PICKING HER NOSE!" After I said that, the entire class burst into laughter. I really didn't mean it, but somebody had to do something. After all, it was pretty disgusting. Jimmy was very embarrassed. I looked at Mr. Morgan to see if he was angry with me. He didn't seem to be angry at all. As a matter of fact, it looked like he was trying to hold back from laughing. What a relief! I got away with

that one. As for Kitty, she was embarrassed
and stopped, but after awhile she was up to
her old tricks again.

CHAPTER 23

Once the excitement had died down, Mr. Morgan decided to teach a social studies lesson. He said that the class was going to review everything they knew about South America. Oh, Boy, that was my area of expertise. I knew all the answers as well as I knew the inside of my cage. I was bubbling over with excitement. School was starting to become lots of fun for me.

The first question the teacher asked was to name the longest river in South America. I knew that, so immediately I shouted, "AMAZON!" The class was shocked when I spoke. Mr. Morgan turned to me and spoke to me like I was an actual student. He must have known I was an intelligent bird and would understand him. He said, "We don't call out answers here, Duncan, we raise our hands." I understood him and said, "Sorry." He smiled and asked the next question. I knew the answer to that one also. I became excited again and started to say, "I know, I know." Again, Mr. Morgan spoke to me, and told me to try to be quiet. Once again, I said, "Sorry." After a child that was called on said the wrong answer, I became excited. It was very hard to control myself. I said, "Wrong! Wrong!" Mr. Morgan was very annoyed by now. He walked up to me and told me if it happened again, he would send me to the corner in the back of the room. Jimmy also told me, "Cool it, Duncan!"

I remained silent for the next few questions. It was very hard for me to do because I knew all the correct answers. A final question was asked. This time I couldn't control myself. I blurted out the answer. The class by now was laughing out of control. Mr. Morgan became angry and put my perch and me in the back of the room. I had just learned my first lesson in school, and was being punished because I couldn't control myself.

In the back of the room, I had the pleasure of sitting next to the wise guy, Marvin. He looked at me and gritted his teeth. He looked real nasty. Most of the kids in Jimmy's class were about ten years old, but not Marvin. He looked about fifteen and needed a shave. I watched him. Since I was no longer allowed to participate in the lesson, I kept a close eye on Marvin. I didn't trust him. This kid was tough. I watched him catch flies with his bare hands and pull their wings off while they were still alive. He would then throw the wingless fly at a nearby student. I could tell he had a killer instinct inside him. Even ROBO PARROT wouldn't mess with this nasty dude.

I knew Marvin was a troublemaker. He must have had a permanent seat in the back of this room. That's where all the trouble makers are found; I should know, because that's where I was, too. I watched Marvin take a straw from his pocket. He then proceeded to tear up small pieces of paper and roll them in his mouth. He then put the wet, rolled papers into the straw. He put the straw to his mouth and blew. The papers shot at other students in the room. He even shot a few at me. This was really becoming annoying. Marvin lost interest in this within a few minutes. Next I watched him draw a picture of the teacher on a piece of paper. He was really quite an artist. He made the teacher with a big head and a bird's body. He even put the figure on a perch like mine. The picture did look very funny. He also put Mr. Morgan's name on the bottom of the paper. He tried to get the other kids' attention and showed them the picture. Snickers could be heard throughout the classroom. Finally, Marvin made the picture into a paper airplane and threw it at Mr. Morgan while his back was turned. Wrong move, Marvin. Mr. Morgan wasn't a very happy camper right now. Remember, he was annoyed at the bird brain next to you? I really didn't think Marvin cared about the consequences of his act.

Well, I was right. Mr. Morgan was angry - very angry - when he opened the paper. He asked who was responsible for it. Naturally, there were no answers. He noted that the entire class would be punished if he didn't find out who drew the picture. There was still total silence. Most of the kids knew Marvin did it, but were afraid to admit it. I'm sure he had his way of dealing with squealers.

Since I put my foot in my mouth many times already today, I figured I might as well do it again. So when Mr. Morgan asked the class who was guilty for the final time, I spoke out. "Marvin did it - Marvin did it!" This made Mr. Morgan furious. He walked up to Marvin and escorted him out of the room to the principal's office. The class loved it. Finally, someone had stood up to Marvin. All of the boys and girls stood up and clapped for me. I was a hero. I opened my mouth and spoke up, but did I put my foot in it again?

CHAPTER 24

By the time Mr. Morgan returned to the classroom, I was surrounded by the entire class. I was quite the celebrity being the first one to stand up to Marvin. I felt like I was a part of the class now.

Mr. Morgan told all the students to take their seats. He looked at me and said, "Well, Duncan, now that you have managed to take over the class, I am going to let you and Jimmy present your report." All right! This was it! It was finally my turn to show everyone what I was made of. The girls and boys were also happy to hear that. They applauded for us.

I was, once again, allowed to stand in front of the room on my perch. Jimmy started to tell a little about some animals of South America. He then proceeded to discuss the life of the Macaw Parrot. He noted that the female laid only two, white eggs. I thought to myself, "No, you're wrong. My egg was blue." But the more I started to think, I realized that my two sisters' eggs were white. I knew that Jimmy was a smart boy, so I figured there must be some truth to his idea about the two, white eggs. I started to think that my egg must have been different because I was special. But if Macaws lay only two eggs, where did mine come from? Maybe I was adopted or maybe my egg got mixed up with another bird's egg. I even started to think weird thoughts that maybe an alien from another planet created my egg and slipped it into my mother's nest. Perhaps there were others like me around sitting back, waiting to take over the world. I knew I was much different from other birds - I was much smarter. My thoughts started to run wild. This was something I would have to check out at a later date.

"Duncan! Duncan! Are you ready?" a voice called. I was so caught up in my thoughts about being an alien from another planet, I wasn't paying attention to Jimmy anymore. Now that I was back in the real world, I remembered that I had to help him with his report. Jimmy explained to the class that his parrot would now answer some questions about South America. I was ready to go. Question after question was fired at me. I answered each one perfectly. There was no doubt in anyone's mind that I was an intelligent bird. Mr. Morgan was extremely impressed with my knowledge of South America. I felt proud and was sure that Jimmy would get an "A" for his report.

The end of the school day had arrived. I considered myself lucky to be the first bird to get an education. As the children got their books ready to go, my eyes became teary thinking about the wonderful day I had. "Life is just great," I thought.

Looking around the room, I noticed that Marvin was back. He had spent most of the day in the principal's office. Knowing him, he probably had a seat there with his name on it. He appeared to look nastier than ever. Most of the children ignored him. A few talked to him. Mr. Morgan asked him if he enjoyed his day with the principal. I, on the other hand, kept my eyes from him. I didn't want anymore trouble. But Marvin walked straight up to my perch and said, "You're a Dead Duck!" What did he mean by that? I wasn't a duck, I was a parrot. And I most certainly wasn't dead. Whatever did he mean by that remark? Jimmy told him to leave me alone, and Mr. Morgan told him to get ready to go home. Marvin did as he was told, but kept staring at me. I knew he was thinking about something mean and nasty.

The ride home on the bus was great. As soon as we sat down, the driver let Jimmy take me out of the box. I was also allowed to sit in the back of the bus with the cool kids. We laughed and joked all the way home. Everyone loved me. Everyone wanted to be my friend. Everyone - except Marvin. He had something in mind for me, and I'm sure it wasn't nice.

As the bus rolled to a stop, I said goodbye to all my friends. The bus driver gave me a pat on the head and said, "Goodbye, Cutie." I gave her a peck on the cheek and said, "Thank you." We stepped off the bus and watched it move down the street. A familiar face watched from a window - the bus moved - it was Marvin. I wondered what he was planning?

CHAPTER 25

Home, sweet home! I had a warm feeling inside of me as we approached our home. I was on top of Jimmy's shoulder feeling very good about myself. I had finally become a parrot of the world. I had made it to school. Things looked different to me. I felt I knew more about the world and the things that lived in it, because I had an education. My education consisted of only a half day at school, but nonetheless, it was an education that I was proud of.

As we walked up the path to the front door of the house, my instincts lit up. I felt as though we were being followed. I couldn't be sure, but I felt like I was being watched. I turned around twice to see if I was correct, but I saw nothing out of the ordinary.

Because we had worked so hard in school, we were both very hungry. Jimmy went straight to the refrigerator and pulled out a tray of food for us to eat for lunch. There we sat, two schoolboys, after finishing a hard day at school. Mom walked in and asked how her two students were. She was pleased when Jimmy told her that everything went great in school.

After lunch, Jimmy put me outside on my perch. I thought more about school as a gentle wind blew all around me. Once again, I sensed something watching me. I looked around the yard and saw nothing. I figured that it was time for a nap, a well deserved nap. Schoolboys do need their sleep. As I dozed off I thought about how successful my life had been.

My eyes opened to the sound of rustling leaves behind me. I turned around to investigate and saw Marvin, who I had snitched on in school, standing behind me with a pillow case extending high, above his head. I didn't have time to fly, so I let out a quick scream, but it was too late. By that time, the sack was around me and tied shut. There I was, inside this sack with no way to get out, cut off from the rest of the world, and my old friend, Marvin, was carrying me down the street to who knows where? What did he want with me? Why was he doing this? I'm sure I would find out sooner or later.

CHAPTER 26

Here I was, bouncing around in a pillow case, being carried through town by the meanest kid in the neighborhood. Obviously, this kid was the type to hold a grudge. I was willing to forgive and forget, but I didn't think he was the "forgiving" type. I was being "birdnapped", and there wasn't a thing that I could do about it. Like it or not, I was at his mercy. I would just have to wait to see what was going to happen, before I thought of an escape plan.

A door slammed, and the bag I was in was thrown on top of a table or something. I landed hard on my beak. Now what? We were where he wanted to be; I wondered what would happen next. I didn't have to wait long to get my answer. The bag was opened, and I was dumped onto the table. Once again, I hit hard like a pile of bricks. "Ouch!" I squawked. "Shut your beak, you stupid bird!" I was told. Marvin looked extra mean and upset. I wasn't going to do anything else to provoke this guy. I believed I had already pushed my luck too far already.

I decided to stand still and wait for him to make the next move. I still wasn't sure what he wanted from me. If he meant to hurt me, he could have done that in my backyard, or, at least, that's what I thought.

89

I was right, Marvin didn't want to harm me. He wanted to teach Jimmy a lesson by holding me for ransom. He said, "You guys made a fool out of me in front of the class, so now I'm going to get even!" I didn't understand why he was so upset. I'm sure this wasn't the first time he made a fool out of himself. The kid wasn't that bright. As a matter of fact, he wasn't very bright at all. I figured, if he wanted to "birdnap" me, there was nothing I could do about it. Why bother to argue with someone with less intelligence than a worm.

I watched Marvin as he wrote a "Ransom Note." It read:

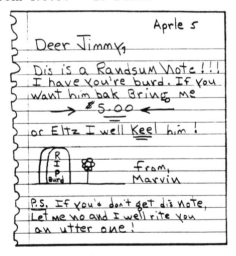

The note was amazing to read. The spelling was terrible. It would be very hard for anyone to read it and figure out what it

meant.   I thought for awhile and figured I
should stay a bit to teach this turkey a
lesson.   It wouldn't take much to do that.
After all, he was a fool, and I was a parrot
with an education.   I watched Marvin finish
the letter and put it into his pocket.   He
told me not to try to escape because he
would be watching me.   He also said that he
was going to deliver the note to Jimmy's
house.   He then locked the door behind him.

After Marvin left, I looked out of a
window.   I saw that I was in a shed.   It had
one window and one door.   It also had a
hole in the roof.   I looked up and saw
daylight coming through from a hole about
the size of a basketball.   How could this kid
think I would be stupid enough to stay here
until he came back.   Well, anyway, I decided
to teach Marvin a lesson when he came
back, but first I had to get things ready.

I flew through the hole in the roof and
saw a tree standing right above it.   I also
noticed a few of my busy bee friends
gathering pollen and bringing it to their
hive.   Guess where the hive was?   It was
hanging directly over the top of the hole in
Marvin's shed.   Now what could I do with
those bees?   I thought that, maybe, they
could help me teach Marvin a lesson.   The
next thing I had to do was to try to figure
out how to keep Marvin in the shed so he
could become acquainted with any new

friends if they happened to pay him a surprise visit. I grabbed a tiny twig, just big enough to fit into the latch on the door. It wasn't that strong, but just strong enough to hold Marvin for awhile.

I heard Marvin coming back so I quickly hid. He removed the pin from the latch, entered the shed, and closed the door behind him. Everything was going perfectly. I flew to the door and inserted the twig into the latch. I could hear Marvin inside the shed looking for me. He kept saying, "Come out here, you dumb bird!" The next thing I did was to fly up into the tree. I reached the bees' nest and started to chew on the part that held it to the branch of the tree. I almost had it off when Marvin shouted, "Where are you, you stupid bird!" I shouted back, "Hello, Marvin!" He saw me through the hole in the roof. He told me to come down or else! With that thought, I bit through the hive and said, "Bombs away!" Marvin watched the hive enter his shed. He didn't realize what it was until the bees started swarming around him. I heard screams coming from the shed. Marvin was banging on the door for someone to let him out. He banged and banged, until the tiny twig in the latch broke loose. Poor Marvin ran down the street, followed by a trail of bees. I think he learned a lesson about bees that day. The lesson was, "Birdnapping, Bees, and Parrots Don't Mix!"

CHAPTER 27

I was as free as a bird. Wait a minute! I was a bird, but I didn't want to be free. All I wanted to do was to go home. How was I going to do that? The neighborhood was new to me and I didn't know my way around it. The only time I flew away from my house was when I was on "Cat Patrol", and that was only as far as the tree in the backyard. Right now, I was lost. I had no idea where I was. The first thing I thought about doing was to fly high and circle the area. I soared like an eagle and looked around, but nothing looked familiar to me. I tried it, again and again, hoping something would look familiar. Then, out of the corner of my eye, I saw a boy far away down the road. "It's Jimmy!" I said excitedly. I raced like a jetliner to where the boy stood. When I got there, I stopped dead in my tracks; I realized that the boy wasn't Jimmy.

What was I going to do? I was hopelessly lost with no way of getting home. A sudden booming noise, followed by drops of rain, put the icing on the cake. Not only was I lost, but it seemed I would be caught in the rain also. The branches of a nearby tree provided me with shelter. A group of crows was already there, but the crows didn't seem to mind sharing their branch. Finally, the rain let up. I looked around the area for anything that looked slightly familiar. Then, I saw it - it was like the light at the end of a tunnel. I remembered Jimmy's parents telling him to do this in case he ever got lost, so, maybe, it applied to me also. I took a deep breath and flew straight to it. I flew to a policeman. The policeman was walking through the neighborhood on his regular beat. He knew the neighborhood better than anyone else. He would know where I lived. I fluttered above his head. I wanted to land on his shoulder, but he was a little nervous about having me around. Instead, I landed on a tree stump and said, "Duncan is lost. Duncan is lost." He took off his hat and scratched his head. He couldn't believe his ears. He thought for a while and said, "OK, Duncan, let's try to find your home." With that, he extended his arm and signaled me to jump on. I felt as though I was in good hands now.

As we walked down the street, I made my way to his shoulder. I felt more comfortable there. He didn't seem to mind. We made several stops, asking people if they had ever seen me before. No one knew anything. Finally, we stopped at the park. The light rain had stopped by now, and some children were playing on the swings.

We approached a group of girls. It wasn't necessary to ask them anything, because a little girl called out my name. "Duncan!" she said, "Where did you come from?" What a relief! This was the same little girl who rescued me on the bus; the same little girl who stuck up for me earlier in the day; the same little girl who knew Jimmy and knew where I lived.

She told the policeman where I lived, and he took me right home. All the way home, I chanted, "Duncan go home - Duncan go home!" I was finally going back to where I should be - "Home-Sweet-Home." The outside world was great, but I preferred the security of my perch, my cage, my house, and my family. The outside world may be a nice place to visit, but I sure wouldn't want to live there.

CHAPTER 28

My family was waiting for me at the doorway of my house by the time I got home. I could tell they were very worried, because their eyes were teary. The policeman explained where he had found me. Mom thanked him for his trouble. Even I said, "Thank you, Officer."

Jimmy took me to the backyard and put me on my perch. He gave me a big hug and said he had been trying to figure out a strange note. He said the note was on my perch, but he couldn't understand any of it except for Marvin's name. He said he was on his way to Marvin's house, when he saw him racing down the street, followed by bees. He said that he figured Marvin was too busy to talk, so he decided to wait until I returned home. He knew that I was smart enough to find my way back.

I didn't think it was important enough to tell Jimmy about my meeting with Marvin, so I yawned and said, "Duncan needs nap. Duncan needs nap." After all, I had been through a lot that afternoon. Jimmy left me on my perch to take a nap. Not much later, I was sleeping like a baby.

I must have slept a few hours because by the time I woke up, it was already dark. I wasn't usually outdoors when it got dark because there were too many unknown creatures of the night that even "ROBO PARROT" didn't know about. I turned towards the house to go inside, when I saw this bright light appear in the sky. The light got brighter and brighter, until it turned the sky into daylight. Suddenly, an object appeared directly overhead and hovered over the yard. It had flashing lights on all sides. The object looked like an alien spaceship. I blinked my eyes in amazement. Never had I seen anything like this before in my life. I had read about them in the newspaper with Dad, but I never thought I would actually see one. I stood as still as a statue, hoping I would go unnoticed. Suddenly, I was shot by a thin beam of light. It didn't hurt. Actually, it felt pretty good. The beam soon shut off, and the spaceship disappeared as quickly as it had appeared. No one would have known it was there, because it all happened so quickly. I figured I shouldn't mention anything about the incident because who would believe me, anyway. After all, there were no such things as spaceships, so I retired into the house after a hard day.

It was dinner time, so I flew to my cage for a bite to eat. As I put my beak into my dish, I accidentally banged my head against the bars of the cage. I always did this because my cage had become sort of small for me. My head didn't hurt so I continued to eat. When I looked up from my dish, I noticed that the same bars on my cage were dented. "That's funny," I said to myself, "I don't remember this dent before." I figured Beastly was up to his old tricks again. After my dinner, I worked my way up the side of the cage by holding onto the bars as I climbed. A funny thing happened though. Each time I grabbed a bar with my beak, it would bend. "What is going on here? My cage is starting to fall apart. They sure don't make cages like they use to!" I said.

I noticed Dad sitting in his chair reading the paper, so I decided to pay him a visit. He was happy to see me and, as always, let me read over his shoulder. Dad asked me to get his pipe for him. I always did this each and every night that he was home. He would kid the family that, when I got big enough, I would be able to fetch his slippers, too. We all knew it was a joke, because how could a parrot carry things as heavy as slippers. I brought his pipe to him and thought that maybe it wouldn't be a bad idea to joke around and try to drag a slipper to him. I left him and said, "Slippers, Duncan get slippers." Dad thought it was cute, and Mom chuckled as I flew off.

I went into the other room and attempted to drag one slipper into the living room. I was sure everyone would get a laugh out of that. But little did I know, I was actually able to lift, not one, but two slippers and fly to the other room with them in my beak. I shocked the family. I shocked myself. Why was I so strong? Was someone slipping me "parrot vitamins" in my food when I wasn't looking? Then it dawned on me - the alien ship - the beam of light! Knowing that beam of light had somehow changed me, I decided to test my strength. I tried lifting everything in the house, from Mom's iron to Dad's bowling ball. I even flew over to the cat and picked it up by its tail, and flew it around the house. The cat screamed for its life, but I was gentle, I let it down easy (on its head). It was amazing! I had the strength of ten men.

My family saw how strong I had become, and figured I should put my newfound strength to good use. Mom knitted me a suit with a fancy "D" on the chest, and everyone called me "SUPER PAR-ROT." Beastly didn't dare mess with me now.

CHAPTER 29

The tiny town of Meadows had been hit by the worst crime wave in its history. The police couldn't keep up with it all. Criminals were getting out of control. Since I was a big hero in the neighborhood, and admired by my many heroic deeds, I could now do something to help the good, honest citizens of my hometown. I took on the job of chief crime fighter. I was known to all as the mighty SUPER PARROT. That was me - SUPER PARROT - strange visitor from another planet with power and abilities far beyond those of normal birds. SUPER PARROT, who could change the course of mighty rivers, bend steel in his bare beak. And who, disguised as Duncan, the Parrot, mild mannered bird from Martin Street, fights a never ending battle for truth, justice, and the American way!

My headquarters had moved from my perch in the backyard to the top of City Hall. I would keep crime in check and protect all the citizens of the town of Meadows. I would simply fly down behind the culprit, snatch him up, and carry him to justice. I had the town cleaned up in a matter of weeks. The crime wave had soon ended. Criminals feared, but respected me. The Mayor had a statue erected in my honor. A parade was held to show the town's appreciation for my heroic deeds.

My family was exceptionally proud of me. I was on the news and was given a medal by the president. Children cheered for me - adults clapped - my fellow birds chirped. I had become the greatest bird in the world. Big Bird, move over - Super Parrot is here!

The phone rang; it was my hotline. The police needed help. Someone had planted a bomb on top of City Hall. They wanted me to dispose of it. It would go off in two minutes. Like a flash of light, I was on my way - Super Parrot to the rescue!

I arrived on the scene with only seconds left. I couldn't disarm the bomb, so I took it high into the sky so no one would be injured when it exploded. Higher and higher I went. Suddenly, without warning, the bomb exploded, sending my battered body down towards the earth. Was this the end of Super Parrot? I hit the ground with a tremendous thud. My beak was broken into pieces. Feathers and flesh had been torn from my body, thanks to the explosion. I was a motionless mass of burnt feathers. Jimmy ran to me and shouted, "Duncan, wake up! Duncan, wake up!" "Super Parrot is here," I said. "Super Parrot?" Jimmy said, "Wake up, Duncan, you silly bird. You're only dreaming. " I opened my eyes and realized where I was - safely on my perch in the backyard where I had been napping. Jimmy was right, it was only a dream. But what a dream it was!

101

CHAPTER 30

Summer vacation had begun. The schools were closed, and the children were free to do the important stuff that could only be done during the summer. School had taken its toll on them, and they needed to unwind and let it all hang out. This was the true meaning of summer - the time children throughout the country lived for. On the other hand, the parents were the ones who dreaded summer vacation. Their kids would constantly be underfoot and getting into mischief. If anyone knew about summer trouble, it was Mom and Dad. This was the time of the year Beastly loved the best. It was his season; a time to be extra annoying; a time to be a bigger pest; a time to do what he did best - BOTHER ME!

One afternoon while I was sunning myself on my perch in the backyard, Beastly casually walked towards me. He was grinning, that "I'm up to something" Beastly grin. As usual, I was very suspicious of him. Beastly didn't have one sneaky bone in his body - he had 206 sneaky bones in his body! As he walked by, I kept an eye on him, just in case he had any funny ideas. Surprisingly enough, he circled the yard and returned into the house. However, just to make sure I noticed him, he said, "So long, Bird Breath," as he disappeared through the doorway. What was he up to? Summer vacation had just begun and Beastly was on the prowl. I wondered when he would strike next.

It didn't take long for me to get my answer. I felt a few drops of rain fall from the sky. The sun was out, so I figured that it was only a sun shower. More and more rain started falling. It felt good. I opened my wings to take advantage of what was happening. I've always said that if opportunity knocks at your door, answer it. This was my opportunity to use the rain to take a quick shower. Well, opportunity not only knocked on my door, it banged and banged. It banged so hard that it broke the door down, because a bucket, not a drop, of water suddenly exploded on me. I was soaked from beak to toe. My feathers were water-logged. They stuck like glue to my body. If the "wet look" was in, I would most certainly have qualified. My feathers also absorbed a great deal of water. I was three times heavier than I should have been. I was so heavy that I could barely hold on to my perch without falling off. Flying was naturally out of the question, so all I did was stay on my perch and try to shake the water from my body. I could only hope that whatever had happened to me would not happen again. Well, history, once again, repeated itself, and another bucket of water hit me and knocked me off of my perch. There I lay, water-logged and helpless on the ground.

I looked up towards an upstairs window and saw good, old Beastly with an empty bucket in his hands. He was grinning from ear to ear. "Beastly," I thought, "you've done it to me again, but it ain't over 'till the fat lady sings!"

CHAPTER 31

The summer vacation had just begun, and Beastly was already up to his old tricks. If this was just the beginning of his so-called pranks, what was going to happen to me for the rest of the summer? I decided then and there that I wouldn't be able to tolerate his mischief and would have to teach him a lesson once and for all. I have to admit that pulling pranks and getting even with Beastly was funny, but when you think about it, pranks can sometimes be dangerous and people can get hurt. If you thought about everything we had done to each other, one of us could really have gotten hurt. For example, when he first bounced me back and forth in the box, or got me drunk, or fed me hot seeds, or tied a string to my leg and spun me around his head - I could have become very sick or even could have died because of someone's weird sense of humor. Even the stuff I did to him - like getting ants down his pants- could have really hurt him. I've always said that revenge is sweet, but there is a point where you can go too far.

The more I thought about the nasty things he had done to me, the more I wanted to really fix him good. I wanted to fix him once and for all so he would never bother me again. This had to be the greatest prank I had ever pulled off, but at the same time, show him that pranks could be dangerous.

I knew Beastly would always sit in the backyard on weekends and read. The summer months meant reading comic books, not regular books, like during school months. Beastly was into Superman and Batman comics. He had stacks of them in his bedroom closet. Nobody was allowed to borrow them, not even Jimmy. Beastly felt very strongly about that. I figured I could set fire to these precious items and teach him a lesson. The consequences of making a fire in his closet occurred to me. A fire might spread throughout the entire house. That idea was definitely out. I would have to come up with some sort of alternate plan. But what? I had a lot of time to think. Too bad I couldn't send Beastly to camp for the summer, or better yet, maybe I could be sent to camp. Maybe I could trap him in a box and have him mailed to Antarctica; or, maybe, I could learn magic and cast a spell on Beastly and turn him into a toad or something. Perhaps I could contact an alien spaceship and have the aliens take him back to their home planet. Thoughts like these continued to run through my mind. I realized none of them would ever come true, but after all, a bird can dream, can't he?

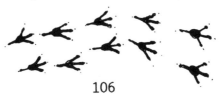

CHAPTER 32

I became quite the celebrity in the neighborhood park during the summer. Jimmy would bring me with him a few days a week. I would sit on his shoulder as we rode his bike. Sometimes we would pretend to be the police chasing after a crook. I would make a sound like a siren warning people to get out of our way. It was funny watching the expressions on people's faces as we roared by. Let's face it, not too many kids have a screaming parrot on their shoulder while they ride their bikes.

Jimmy and I weren't the only members of our family at the park, Beastly was also there with his friends. While Jimmy played ball or rode his bike, Beastly would hang around with other Beastly-like kids. These kids were exactly like our friend Beastly: they had no ambition to do anything but hang out all day, and they were very obnoxious to each other and anyone that passed by. Why do teenagers act like this? Boy, I'm glad we birds don't become obnoxious when we hit our teens.

I did a lot of exploring in the park. Jimmy let me fly around to keep myself busy. I would explore the trees, visit the wildlife, and entertain the children. I was a one bird show. The little kids and their mothers loved to watch me do my stuff.

They especially liked to hear me talk. I would sing and talk all day long. Everyone knew me by name. The little kids would scream, "There's Duncan, let's go see Duncan!" Who needed Disneyland with Donald and Mickey, when you could go to the park and see Duncan, the talking parrot.

The older kids, along with Beastly, were a strange bunch. Sometimes they would make fun of the younger kids, or try to show off in front of the girls. I couldn't understand why they would do this. In my opinion, if you wanted to show off or impress someone, you would act sophisticated and intelligent, but these guys acted real stupid and did dumb things, like wrestle on the ground, throw things at each other, or even throw things at the girls they were trying to impress. The girls mostly looked at them in disgust and walked away. I just can't understand human teenagers. It's too confusing.

One day, while Jimmy and I were biking through the park, we noticed Beastly and his friends. They were up to something because they were trying to hide what they were doing. As we rode past, we noticed Beastly with a cigarette in his hand, and it was lit. He walked over to us and threatened to hurt us if anything was mentioned about this at home. He looked at me and warned Jimmy that the "Bigmouth Bird", had better not say anything either. Jimmy assured him that we didn't care anyway, and we wouldn't say a word. I wasn't too sure about that. As much as I disliked Beastly, he was a member of the family, and smoking was bad for his health. Big Bird taught me that when I was a young bird. I cared about Beastly's health, so I had to figure out a way to try to make him stop smoking. At the same time, I didn't want to squeal on him either, because Jimmy did make a promise.

It troubled me a lot knowing that Beastly had developed a bad habit which wasn't good for him. I wondered how I could stop him, or at least, let Mom and Dad know what he was doing. I was sure they would know how to deal with him. I set my bird brain to work on finding a plan to stop him, at any cost. Strange as it may sound, I was actually trying to help Beastly. It was hard for me to believe what I was thinking, "Me, Duncan - helping Beastly?"

CHAPTER 33

Once again, the weekend was upon us, and I could be found on my perch in the backyard taking in the sunshine. I just loved to be outdoors on a sunny day. As I stood there, preening my feathers, my buddy Beastly, strolled past me. He gritted his teeth at me and said, "Back off, Eagle Lips!" He always had something nasty to say to me, but I was used to it. I tried to tolerate him as much as I could.

Beastly had a magnifying glass in his hand. I wondered what he was up to. I kept a close eye on him just in case I was his next victim. He didn't bother me, though. He proceeded to shine the magnifying glass on a nearby anthill. He was using the sun's light, which was shining through the glass, to burn the ants as they came out of their hole. I remembered the science lesson Jimmy's teacher taught when I visited school. He said a magnifying glass makes things bigger when you look through it. He also said that if sunlight shines through a magnifying glass, the light will become stronger, and it may even burn a surface. Beastly was applying his science skill creatively, but at the expense of the poor ants coming from their home. He snickered and laughed as he terrorized the ants. The poor things didn't stand a chance against the big bully. All I could do was to sit back and watch. Beastly soon lost interest in his work and put the magnifying glass on a nearby table. He then sat down with his comic book and started to read. I noticed he had a pack of cigarettes in his back pocket. There were also matches with a half open cover sticking up. This gave me an idea - if Beastly liked to smoke, I would help him smoke. I would let the world know he smoked, and I wouldn't have to say a single word.

The first thing I had to do was to get the magnifying glass without him knowing. This wasn't too difficult because he was really involved with another chapter of his Batman comic. I fluttered unnoticed to the table and picked up the glass with my feet. I then returned to my perch. Beastly didn't notice a thing. In fact, he was talking to the comic. He said, "Get that creep, Batman!" I then turned the magnifying glass towards Beastly's back pocket - you know- the one with the matches. The sun was shining very brightly that day, and, in no time, the sun's rays shining through the magnifying glass made the matches hotter and hotter. Suddenly, a flame appeared in Beastly's pocket. Then the entire pack of matches burst into flames. It didn't take him long to realize that his pants were on fire. He jumped up from his chair and started smacking his back pocket, while he screamed, "Help! Help! Help! My pants are on fire!" Mom and Dad heard the noise and ran outdoors. By this time, Beastly was in the middle of the yard, bouncing on his rear end, trying to put out the fire. I felt the need to help him, and noticed a hose attached to a water sprinkler close to where he was jumping around. So I quickly flew to the faucet and twisted it with my feet. The sprinkler came on and helped put out the fire. Beastly was soaked, but his pants were still smoking. By this time, Mom and Dad were already outside wondering what was going on. I turned off the sprinkler so they could investigate. There stood Beastly soaked from head to toe, trying to take the contents out of his back pocket. He tried to hide them in a nearby bush. Dad caught notice of the burnt cigarette package and demanded to know what was going on. Beastly confessed to having matches and cigarettes in his pocket. Mom was very upset about her son smoking and almost started to cry. Dad just shook his head. The three of them then went into the house.

I was surprised not to hear screaming and yelling. Instead Mom and Dad talked calmly to Beastly about the hazards of smoking, and how bad it was for his health. Surprisingly enough, Beastly listened, and to this day, he hasn't smoked a single cigarette. His friends who smoked tried to tease him and call him "Chicken" when he refused to take a cigarette, but he stuck to his promise to Mom and Dad that he would never smoke again. Way to go, Beastly! There's hope for you yet!

I felt bad about doing what I did to Beastly, but I was very pleased with its results. I guess I'm not a mean bird after all, even to Beastly. I think he realized that I was responsible for setting his pants on fire, but he never tried to get even. As a matter of fact, he didn't bother me anymore after that. His pranks were history; maybe because he grew up, or perhaps, he was grateful that I helped him quit smoking. Whatever the reason, we got along fairly well after that. I eventually called him by his correct name, "Marvin". I couldn't call him Beastly anymore, because he became a nice person. Marvin and I became silent friends; we never admitted we liked each other, but deep down inside, we really did. Occasionally we teased each other for old times sake - he called me Bird Breath and I called him Beastly. After all, why should we disappoint everyone - it was our little secret.

CHAPTER 34

The dream I had about the alien spaceship and Super Parrot recurred over the summer months. Sometimes, during the night, I would find myself screaming, "Super Parrot to the rescue!" Why was I bothered by this dream? Did it mean something to me? Some experts say that when you dream about something, you are actually bothered by a real problem. Did I have a problem? The only problem I had was Beastly, but that problem had been worked out.

It suddenly dawned on me why this dream occurred over and over again. It must have had something to do with Jimmy's report on Macaw Parrots. He said that Macaw's eggs are white, not blue, which was the color of the egg from which I was hatched. Macaws lay two eggs, not three. My egg was one of three eggs. Things just didn't make sense, and I was troubled by the question, "Was I, or wasn't I, a real Macaw Parrot?" I knew I was much smarter than normal birds. Silly thoughts popped into my head about an alien egg put into my mother's nest. Super Parrot was a strange visitor from another planet - could that be true about me? I soon dismissed these thoughts and made a promise that I would find out the truth about myself, no matter what the consequences. I did look like a

Macaw, there was no doubt about that, so I started my research about the Macaw.

Jimmy had a book about birds in his room. I was certain he would let me borrow it to find a few answers. I found him reading in his room, and I proceeded to say, "Duncan look at bird book. Duncan look at bird book." He knew I liked to see pictures of my feathered friends, so he found the book and opened it for me. I turned the pages carefully with my beak, until I came to the section on Macaws. There were several pictures. One picture, in particular, looked exactly like me. I read the page as carefully as I could. It said that Macaws lay two white eggs. Well, there was no doubt that Jimmy was correct on his information when he did his report. Now what should I do? Where can I go from here? I turned a few more pages and came to a section about birds that laid their eggs in other birds' nests. As I read on, there were two birds, in particular, that interested me: the Cow Bird and the Cuckoo. Both of these birds would lay their eggs in another bird's nest. The new mother bird would then raise the baby bird as her own. It didn't seem to matter to her at all. Did this, maybe, happen to me? Did my real mother lay her egg in a Macaw's nest? I read on further and was stunned by what I discovered: the Cuckoo's egg was blue. Oh, no! My mother was a Cuckoo! That means my father was a Cuckoo. That leaves no other explanation - I must also be a Cuckoo. Duncan, the Cuckoo Bird. That didn't have a nice sound like Duncan, the Macaw Parrot. The only time I had actually seen a Cuckoo was on television. They were usually dopey birds that were constantly confused and did silly things. Mostly they were found in Cuckoo clocks, and would stick their heads out every hour and half hour and say, "Cuckoo, Cuckoo." What a strange bird the Cuckoo was. Why, of all the birds in the world, did I have to turn out to be a Cuckoo?

I left Jimmy's room and flew to my perch. I stood there feeling very sorry for myself. In a few short minutes, I went from being a distinguished Macaw Parrot, to a Cuckoo Bird. How humiliating. But the more I thought about it, the more I figured, "So what! Who cares if I'm a Cuckoo or a Macaw - a bird should be judged for what he is inside." That part of me hadn't changed. I was still the same bird I was a few minutes ago. Nobody could take that from me. I was, and always will be, Duncan, the bird, no matter what happened. I'm sure Jimmy would still love me. Mom and Dad wouldn't care. Even my new friend, Marvin (Beastly), wouldn't be upset. So why should I be bothered by such a trivial event. Life was too short, and I was going to give it my best shot.

CHAPTER 35

If I was destined to be a Cuckoo Bird, I made up my mind to be the best Cuckoo Bird ever. As a Cuckoo, I would make the other Cuckoos proud of me. I really didn't know much about the Cuckoo, except for what I saw on television. Acting silly and being confused wasn't very impressive, so I decided to play the part of the Cuckoo in the clock.

I practiced my Cuckoo sound until I was very good at it. I was now ready to become a true Cuckoo. On each hour and half hour I would say, "Cuckoo! Cuckoo!" I was very exact with my time, and Dad would be able to set his watch by my calls. I was very good at what I did, but something seemed to be missing. I decided then to give the actual time every half hour. I would say, "Cuckoo! Cuckoo! It's 7:00," or I would say, "Cuckoo! Cuckoo! It's 2:30." The family loved my time reminders. I truly was a terrific Cuckoo.

I soon became obsessed with calling out the time. I would call out every fifteen minutes, and it got much worse - I would start to call out every five minutes. The family was concerned about my strange behavior. They figured I was just going through a phase and would soon grow out of it. They hoped things would get better, not worse. Jimmy was very worried about the whole situation. He spoke to me like a big brother, asking why I was always giving the time. I told him, "Duncan is a Cuckoo. My egg was blue." I proceeded to call out the time again and again. I just couldn't help it. Jimmy went to his room and pulled out the book I was reading. It didn't take him long to realize what was in that little bird brain of mine. He made a phone call and told the person on the other end of the line that we were on our way. "Who was he talking to?" I thought. Jimmy told me to hop on his shoulder, and we were on our way.

The bike ride was interesting. Instead of a police siren on his shoulder, Jimmy had a Cuckoo Bird shouting out the time. People were impressed with me as we passed. I could see them checking their watches and nodding their heads in agreement. I truly was the best Cuckoo Bird there ever was. I was proud to be Duncan, the Cuckoo.

CHAPTER 36

I wondered where Jimmy was taking me as we quickly sped down the street to our destination. I continued my time announcements as we rode. Finally, we coasted to a stop and found ourselves in front of my old place of residence - we were in front of the pet store on Howard Boulevard.

A strange feeling entered my body as we walked through the front door. The smell I grew up with filled my beak with memories of my early birdhood. I wanted to see my parents and the place where I hatched from my egg. I didn't care anymore about proving myself to be a "Super Cuckoo." I just wanted to relive my early birdhood memories.

I looked at Jimmy and said, "Duncan see Mommy. Duncan see Mommy." He understood and walked me to the birds' cages. There, in front of me, was the cage I was hatched in. My parents were still there. They were surprised when I appeared in front of them. My mother recognized me immediately - mothers are like that; they always seem to remember their children, no matter how they change. We exchanged greetings and kissed each other through the bars of the cage. It was great seeing my parents again.

The store owner came over to the cages to talk with Jimmy. I noticed that my mother was sitting on three eggs. She shouldn't lay three eggs; Macaws lay only two eggs. One positive thing, however, was that all three eggs were white, but we were still back where we started. I became nervous and started giving the time of day again. "Relax, Duncan," Jimmy said, "I'm sure there's a logical explanation for this." I listened as Jimmy asked the store owner why this particular Macaw had three eggs in her nest, when there should only be two. The store owner was also confused. He said that this particular female had also laid three eggs the last time. He also said it was the strangest thing he had ever seen.

The story sounded logical. A female could lay three instead of two eggs each time. So what if she was a little different than other Macaws. But what about the blue egg? There was still no logical explanation about that. I said, "Duncan's egg was blue. Duncan's egg was blue." Jimmy explained what I meant and the store owner just laughed. How could this guy laugh about a thing like that? He said that he remembered a painter, who was painting behind the cages, accidentally spilled some blue paint into one of the cages. He continued to say that one of the eggs became covered with paint. He tried to clean it off, but he couldn't. There was no harm done, and nobody was upset, so he figured he would leave it blue. Nobody was upset? How could he say that? I was upset! This was very important to me! He also remembered the little show-off bird that came out of the blue egg. Then he looked straight at me and winked.

I never heard a story with a happier ending. I was finally convinced that I was a real Macaw Parrot. There were no doubts about that. The number of eggs - the blue egg - everything fit together. I was happier than I had ever been. Jimmy was pleased with the store owner's answers and thanked him for his help. I said good-bye to my parents and also thanked the store owner. I could see he was very impressed with how smart I had become.

The ride home was probably the best ride I ever had. There I stood, on Jimmy's shoulder, a proud Macaw Parrot, and no one would ever be able to take that away from me. I may have been a cuckoo a few days before, but today had changed that. Today I was happy to be alive.

CHAPTER 37

Some people may say, "Life is for the birds." I never really understood what that meant, but my life as a bird was great. I had a family that loved me, and kids in the neighborhood looked forward to seeing me. I had made friends with Beastly, and things always seemed to go my way. If life is for the birds, I'll take it - after all, I am a bird.

After all the help Jimmy had given me when I was a younger bird, I decided it was my turn to help him. He was such a considerate and unselfish boy, so I wanted to do something nice for him. He had a summer newspaper route, and he would deliver his papers everyday around noon. Helping him deliver newspapers would save him time, and enable us to spend more time together. So the next time he was ready to start his deliveries, I was right there on his shoulder, ready to help. I said, "Let Duncan help. Let Duncan help." Jimmy thought the idea was terrific. I knew we would make a great team. The newspapers weren't more than a few pages thick, because we did live in a small town. This was lucky for me, because I wouldn't be able to carry much more weight than that, anyway.

We were off to a great start. I would ride on Jimmy's shoulder shouting, "Paper!

Paper! Get your Paper!" He would then drive to the front of a house on his route. We had a great system: Jimmy would fold the paper and hand it to me; I would pick it up with my feet, fly to the front porch, and drop it there.

The customers appreciated this delivery system, because other paperboys would throw the papers into the bushes or on top of the roof. I, on the other hand, would always drop it on the porch. Sometimes the customers would already be waiting for their papers. I would then drop the newspapers into their hands. Occasionally, a cat would be sitting on the porch. You'll never guess where I dropped the paper then! One time, Mrs. Jones, a lady down the street, tried to catch the paper. I flew straight over her and dropped it. She wasn't wearing her glasses and misjudged it. The paper hit her square in the nose. Lucky for her it wasn't the Sunday paper, which was twice as heavy. It might have broken her nose.

What a team! We worked great together. People called us the Dynamic Duo, Paperboy and Paperbird. Eat your heart out Batman and Robin. Jimmy and Duncan are taking over!

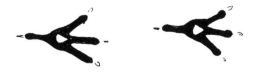

CHAPTER 38

One day, after delivering newspapers, Jimmy and I met up with some of his friends. Sometimes we would ride our bikes through the park, or around the neighborhood. Today, though, his friends wanted to ride through an area of town that was OFF-LIMITS to everyone. This part of town was a deserted building sight that ran out of money a few years before. The words "NO TRESPASSING" were posted on signs all around to keep people from danger. Many uncovered holes were found around the area, huge rocks were waiting to topple over, and the ground was soft in some places. Any sensible person would have seen that it was dangerous, and they should "KEEP OUT!"

The other kids had it set in their minds that they were going to go dirt biking in this area. You know little boys. It was the cool thing to do. Jimmy didn't want to enter and tried to convince the others that it was unsafe, but they started teasing him and called him "Chicken". Can you imagine a group of ten year olds clucking away? I don't know why kids do that. Jimmy tried to resist, but the pressure was too much for him, and he went along with the group. I knew this meant trouble, and we would soon see what we were getting involved in.

The group found an opening through the fence where they could fit their bikes. The boys then proceeded to pedal up and down the hills as fast as they could. There didn't seem to be any danger yet, but the road ahead seemed to get rougher and rougher. About ten minutes of travel time brought us to the top of a high hill. It was a long, rocky way down to the bottom. The boys hesitated, but they soon went down, one after the other. It was finally our turn. Jimmy was leery of the hill. He knew only a foolish person would attempt to race down it, but if everyone else made it, he figured he could do it too.

Down, down, down we went. The wheels of the bike spun faster and faster. The bumps we were hitting made the entire frame of the bike jump higher and higher. I had all I could do to balance myself on Jimmy's shoulder. Suddenly, we hit this huge rock in the middle of the path. The front wheel of the bike snapped at the frame, and there we were flying through the air as the bike turned upside down. I was able to jump off and flutter to safety, but poor Jimmy flew with the bike and landed on a pile of rocks. When the dust cleared, Jimmy was lying on top of a pile of jagged rocks. He must have struck his head, because he wasn't moving. There were cuts all over his body. There was a huge gash on his forehead. I immediately flew to him and tried to see if he was conscious. I

called, "Jimmy! Jimmy!" but he didn't answer.
By this time, his friends had seen what had
happened. They rushed toward him to help.
One kid put his ear by Jimmy's nose and
said that he was still breathing. They tried
waking him, but it was no use. I didn't
know what to do. My best friend in the
whole world was lying helplessly in front of
me, and I couldn't do anything to help him.

I started to think of all the help Jimmy
had given me in the past, and I couldn't
help him at all, now that he needed it. I
felt totally useless. His friends didn't know
what to do either. They started shouting at
one another and tried to blame each other
for the accident. These guys would be no
help. It was entirely up to me to do
something about it. I thought for a moment
and then reacted. I flew straight into the
air like a jet and headed towards town. I
had to find help somewhere.

When I arrived in town, it looked like
it was deserted. I flew around, not knowing
what I was looking for, but there, in front
of me was help - it was a police car. I
raced to it and landed on its hood. The
policeman inside the car opened his door and
came over to me to investigate. I recognized this policeman: he was the one that
helped me find my way home when I was
lost. I hoped he would remember me. He
said, "Hello, Duncan. Are you lost again?" I
repeated over and over, "Jimmy is hurt.

Help! Jimmy is hurt. Help!" The policeman knew my reputation in the neighborhood and said for me to lead him to Jimmy. I was so relieved he understood what I was trying to say. He radioed in and told an ambulance to stand by for an emergency.

I flew ahead of the police car. He was right behind me, flashing his lights and sounding his siren. We were soon at the building site. The policeman radioed again and told the ambulance of the location. He then followed me to where Jimmy was hurt. I was surprised that the police car was able to travel over that rocky path, but I was glad he could do it for Jimmy's sake.

When we reached Jimmy the boys were shocked to see the policeman behind me. They ran to him and explained what had happened. A few minutes later, the ambulance arrived and took Jimmy straight to the hospital. I had done my part to help Jimmy. Now it would be up to the doctors at the hospital.

As the ambulance pulled away, I felt relieved that Jimmy was in safe hands, yet I had a deep concern for his health. Was he going to be OK? I didn't want to think about it if he wasn't. I could only hope that he would be alright. The policeman got more information from the boys and radioed to the station to notify Mom and Dad that there was an accident. I would hate to receive a phone call like that. I wondered if Mom would be able to handle the bad news.

The policeman took me into his car and drove me home. There was no one there by the time we arrived because they were already at the hospital, so the policeman put me on my perch and patted my feathers. He said, "Duncan, you are a very brave parrot. You did a very nice thing for Jimmy today. You may have saved his life." He also said that things would workout, and that Jimmy would be home in no time at all. "See you around the neighborhood, Duncan," he said, and he left the yard. As I stood on my perch, I thought about all the good times Jimmy and I had together. He was my best friend, and I couldn't bear the thought of losing him. Memories of our meeting flashed across my mind. He would be fine, I was sure of it. He'd probably be home in a few days. I could only hope that I was right.

CHAPTER 39

It seemed like almost an eternity as I waited for the family to return home. I needed to know how Jimmy was, and if he was going to be OK. Crazy thoughts kept going through my head. The more I thought about them, the more worried I became. Finally, I heard the car turn into the driveway. I was already at the front door by the time the family had entered the house. Before anyone could say anything, I started shouting, "Is Jimmy OK? Is Jimmy OK?" Dad walked up to where I was standing, and, with a smile on his face, said, "Jimmy is going to be just fine, Duncan." I heard this and started shouting, "Fine! Fine! Jimmy is fine!" I was so excited, my best friend in the whole world was going to be fine. Dad also said that Jimmy would have to stay in the hospital for a few days.

Mom walked up to me and gave me a kiss on the beak and told me how brave I was. She told me that she met my friend, the policeman, and he explained what I had done for Jimmy. She was so thankful that her eyes started to fill up with tears. She gave me another kiss on the beak. Even Beastly complimented me on my heroic deed. Dad told me I had to be the smartest bird in the entire world, and he was proud I was a member of his family.

It made me feel good that everyone appreciated what I had done for Jimmy, but that didn't seem to matter to me. I was just thankful he was safe and sound, and I was more than happy to do what I could for a friend. After all, if you can't depend on a friend to help you when you're in trouble, who can you depend on? Jimmy was my friend, and I would do anything for him.

CHAPTER 40

The next morning the family was getting ready to pay Jimmy a visit in the hospital. When I found out, I jumped around and said, "Duncan visit Jimmy. Duncan visit Jimmy." Mom heard me and tried to explain that pets weren't allowed in the hospital. There was that "Pet" rule again. Pets can't ride on a bus, and they can't visit anyone in a hospital. What a bunch of stupid rules. What were they afraid of? I don't bite! I don't make a mess on the floor! Who makes these stupid rules anyway? I became angry and shouted, "No fair! No fair!" Mom said to calm down and said she would tell Jimmy that I missed him. A lot of good that would do. I needed to see him. We were a team. We needed each other. You can't keep pals apart.

I think Beastly knew what I was thinking, and he winked at me. He signaled for me to come upstairs with him. Should I trust him, or what? He had been very nice to me since I set his pants on fire. Would now be the time for him to get even? I decided to trust him. The last time I trusted him, I wound up with a mouthful of hot pepper seeds. Thinking this over, I followed him upstairs anyway. Was this going to be a major mistake? The next thing I knew I was shoved into a tiny box by Beastly. Now what had I gotten myself into? Would this finally be the end of me? Only time would tell.

I felt like I was being carried around. I didn't know what to expect. I heard voices most of the time, but I chose not to say anything. Suddenly, I felt this funny feeling in my stomach. It felt as though I was going up into the air and back down again. Going up wasn't too bad, but coming down made me feel sick to my stomach. When the weird feeling stopped, I felt like I was being carried again. Then I heard sounds and voices. "Was this my final destination?" I said to myself.

Suddenly, without warning, the box opened, and there, holding me in his hands, was Jimmy. I was in the hospital. Beastly must have carried me there in the box. Jimmy's face lit up like the sun when he saw me. He wasn't the only happy camper here. I was excited and kept saying, "Duncan visit Jimmy. Duncan visit Jimmy." Mom looked at Beastly and shook her head. She told him to keep an eye out for the nurse before we got thrown out of the room. He winked at me and stood near the door. Beastly turned out to be alright, after all. Jimmy was so happy that he kissed my beak, so I gave him a peck on the cheek.

We were two of the happiest friends in the world. We would continue to be friends for the rest of our lives. No one would be able to separate us from each other. There were more adventures waiting for us, many more places to explore, and trouble waiting down the road. People all over the world would depend on our help. The weak needed our strength, bullies needed taming, and cats needed scaring. What did the future have in store for us with all of this hanging over our heads? Well that, my friend, is another story.